— ANGELVERSE 1 —

HIGANBANA

JAKE VANGUARD

Contents

For myself and still being alive.

Content Warnings

Higanbana includes but is not limited to: Alcohol consumption, Angst, Blasphemy, Blood, Body Horror, Chronic Pain, Cigarettes, Depression, Eating Disorder, Explicit sex, Family trauma, Gender & body dysphoria, Hypothermia, Gun violence, Manipulation, Near-Death Experience, Self-Harm, Sexual assault, Side character death, Suicidal thoughts & actions, Torture, Transphobia/Transphobic Slurs, Traumatic Memory Loss, C-PTSD, Vomiting

If you have any questions or anything to add, please feel free to email Jake at jake.vanguard.author@gmail.com.

Falling

Endless falling from Heaven.

What happened?

Why was it happening to him?

He remembered Maalik...

Earth came closer every second.

His wings were burning away, as were his angelic robes.

His body hurt like it never had before.

Why did it have to happen to him?

Burning agony and sadness filled him.

Seeing the Earth still coming closer, his arms formed a shield in front of his face.

Crashing onto the ground, he left a big mark.

He dragged his aching body into a more secure spot.

No more strength, no more motivation.

His gaze wandered toward the sky.

And a single tear rolled down his cheek.

His home...lost forever.

CHAPTER ONE

After The Fall

AUGUST 29TH, 2023

He'd done it again. Nathaniel could feel the fresh burn on his shoulder. He was surprised there was still some space left. He didn't know why they kept doing this to him, but he'd accepted his fate. His boyfriend, Daniel, was no different than his own father.

With a sigh, he looked around and checked if someone was watching him before he crossed the fence corralling the old, abandoned factory. It was one of his favorite places to be. Halfway broken gray walls surrounded him, the smell of spray paint from graffiti artists always lingering.

The solitary space made him feel safe from the clutches of his father and his boyfriend. Although today, something was different, a nagging feeling in the back of his mind that he wasn't alone for once—but he didn't care much. What was the worst that could happen? Nothing could be worse than being home and in Daniel's grasp.

He just wanted to be far away from that, somewhere Daniel didn't know about, and listen to some music, maybe draw a bit. Whenever he felt lost in his life, like he did that day, he would seek solace in drawing, practicing his skill for as long as he had time to spare.

When he arrived at his usual spot, he threw his backpack to the chipped ground and sat down on the cracked stone floor. His back leaned against the cool wall behind him. The sunshine never found its way into the room, despite the broken roof.

After a moment of just closing his eyes and taking in the soothing coldness on his back, he got his sketch book and pencil out of his backpack. Today, his creativity was as lacking, as his will to live; he felt twisted and unfocused. Without thinking much and just to keep his hands occupied, he started sketching. It took some time for him to realize what he was drawing—was it an angel?

"Bullshit," he grumbled. "There's no such thing as angels."

So why should he be drawing one? He didn't believe in gods, angels, demons, or the like. If anything higher existed, why was there so much pain in this world? Why didn't they do shit about it?

With a deep exhale, he leaned back again, allowing his gaze to wander around, to try to find some other inspiration for a sketch. Anything was better than an *angel* of all things. He'd rather sketch the bright graffiti on the wall opposite of him, although it was just a name tag. But the only interesting thing he found were...feet? Why was there a pair of naked feet? He frowned and put his sketch book and pencil down on the ground, then got up. His curiosity was piqued, even though he knew full well it was a dumb idea to approach a stranger in this factory.

He crept closer to the corner, silent on his feet. A person must be hidden behind the wall. Nate was careful, since it could be a junkie or a crazy person, just waiting to attack and rob him. Carefully, he looked around the corner to find a man lying on the ground, completely naked. *What the...?*

The man appeared to be unconscious, but Nate still kept a watchful eye on him, in case it was just a ruse. If he was about to be robbed, Nate wouldn't even fight. He was too tired for this shit, too done with life.

He let his eyes wander over the still body, doing his best not to let his gaze be drawn to the person's private parts. He was a decent guy after all. The stranger was tall, and his skin was almost shockingly pale, as was his hair. When Nate looked at the man's lips, they were soft and full, with a slight tint of redness to them that made him wonder if they'd be warmer than the rest of his body. Everything about him seemed perfect. He almost looked like an angel. No, it couldn't be. Nate shook his head, pushing these silly thoughts away, and focused on this man again. At least he didn't look like a junkie or gang member.

"Hey, dude, wake up." Still vigilant, Nate crouched down next to the stranger and shook his shoulder a little bit, hoping he would wake up like this. Even with that minimal touch, Nate noticed how cold and clammy his skin was. "Come on. Here's not the best place to sleep," he insisted, and in doing so, he managed to at least get a slight reaction out of the stranger—a low groan and fingers twitching.

As he waited for another reaction, his hand retracted again, and he watched the stranger's face until, finally, his eyes lazily opened. Nate had never seen eyes like this before. They were blazing golden. Nathaniel blinked and looked at them again, but now he could only see a golden gleam fading away, revealing dark green eyes with some golden sparkles in them. Had he imagined it? That must be it. No one could have eyes like that, not naturally.

"You're awake, that's good," Nate said. "How are you? Are you alright?"

A wave of questions overcame him suddenly. Did he need to take him to the hospital? Was he lost? Or maybe he was still coming down from a high. Nathaniel had never done drugs himself, but he had friends who did, so he'd seen his fair share of high-off-their-ass druggies. But this guy appeared more lost than high, if he was being honest. He knew that look in the stranger's eyes—not from his drugged-up friends...from himself. It was the same loneliness that darkened his own vision more times than he'd like to admit.

The pale man closed his eyes for a moment, then looked up into the sky. Nate followed his gaze but could see nothing out of the ordinary. So why, then, did the way he looked up into the sky make Nate's chest feel too tight? Like he was mourning a loss so colossal that it had changed his entire existence? Like his eyes, his soul, were about to crack open from sorrow and pain, drenching his heart with sadness so palpable he was unsure who it belonged to.

"Where am I?" the man asked, his voice a mere whisper.

"We're at the abandoned factory." Everyone in the city knew about it.

"Which factory?"

"The one in Stamdon, of course. What's going on with you? Are you okay?" Why did this guy not even know which city he was in? How much had he partied the night before?

As the stranger let out a choked sound that felt like neither a sob nor a chuckle, Nate watched as his gaze drifted to the sky again. Now, that he was taking a closer took, he could tell that the stranger's cheeks were stained with dried tears.

"I really am on Earth," the stranger said in disbelief. "They actually threw me out."

What the fuck was this guy talking about? Obviously, they were on Earth. Where else would they be?

The stranger looked at him again with his piercing green eyes. "I'm Raziel, formerly Archangel, keeper of secrets, and now apparently a fallen angel."

CHAPTER TWO

Heart Of Gold

AUGUST 29TH, 2023

"Raziel? Seriously?" Nate scoffed. "You're supposed to be an angel? Oh, sorry, fallen angel."

What was wrong with this guy? Whatever he was on, he'd obviously taken too much. He definitely had angelic looks, though, so Nate could understand why this guy was imagining that shit.

"I know it's a lot for a human mind to understand," Raziel said. "I also don't care if you believe me or not. It doesn't change what I am." Slowly, and with a wince, Raziel sat up, revealing yet another thing backing up his crazy talk—wounds on his shoulders, large enough to be the remains of wings.

"You should see a doctor for these," Nate said. "Doesn't look good. Can I call someone to pick you up?"

Now Raziel looked at him as if he'd lost his mind. "I don't know anyone on Earth. I have no idea where to go or what to do now, but thanks for listening."

Great, now this idiot was getting cynical. Made it so much easier and better.

"Okay, okay, if you don't have anyone or anywhere to go, you can stay at my place until you figured it out."

What was he saying? Why was he offering this guy a place to crash? Was it the look in his eyes, that same melancholy wistfulness Nate felt deep in his core?

And there was another problem, too. The guy was naked, which might be a bit suspicious. Although his own clothes wouldn't fit Raziel, his boyfriend's should.

"Stay here," he said. "I'll get you some clothes. You can't walk around like this."

Nate stuffed his things back inside his backpack, then hurried to his house. It wasn't far away, so it took only fifteen minutes to reach the one-room apartment. The smell of old smoke still lingered, despite Nate's frantic efforts to get rid of the stink, but neither airing the rooms nor a deodorizing spray had helped much. Instead, it had concocted a nauseating mixture of fresh lavender scent and the reek of Daniel's cigarettes and burned in his nose.

It was yet another reason to hurry, to leave his drawing utensils on the desk. Thought after thought raced through his mind—who was this stranger, why was he at the factory, naked and with these wounds, and why did he seem so lost and broken? They distracted him from the panic the cigarette reek always sparked inside him.

Nate packed a shirt, underwear, and some trousers in the backpack and hoped Daniel wouldn't learn about this anytime soon. It would only end with more scars and pain, like every time he disappointed his boyfriend in any way.

He was back at the factory about forty minutes later, finding Raziel in the same spot where he left him, now sitting and leaned back against a wall. It must hurt with the wounds on his back, but Raziel didn't appear to be fazed by it.

"Doesn't your back hurt?" Nate wondered. He had seen the wounds, and they looked pretty painful.

Raziel smiled at him faintly, before staring at the sky once again. "It does. But no more than the rest of my body."

"Here, put this on and then let's go. We should get these wounds cleaned."

Raziel looked at him for a moment, before he nodded and got up, revealing he was at least ten centimeters taller than Nathaniel. His assumption, that Daniel's clothes would fit, came true as Raziel put them on. It was wrong seeing another person in his boyfriend's clothes, but right now it wasn't like they had much of a choice.

"Can you walk?"

Raziel looked at him for a moment before taking one step after the other. He was unsteady, but at least he could walk. Slowly, Nate walked next to the want-to-be-angel, thinking about what he'd said. He didn't actually believe this guy was a fallen angel. But if he was telling the truth, why had he fallen? What happened? Heaven probably didn't expel angels for small sins. What had Raziel done to deserve getting kicked out?

Nate shook his head. What was he even thinking? It wasn't real. It was a fantasy, some weird shit Raziel—assuming that was his real name, though it probably wasn't—had told him.

They were much slower than Nate had been on his own, and they drew some attention from people on the street, but most didn't care. People around here were used to the hungover walk home, be it from alcohol or drugs. It wasn't out of the ordinary.

Around them, houses stood close to each other, a sea of grays and browns and beiges, with a little green in between. No one cared for plants; they were only used for dogs to shit in, and the smell of one pile baking under the sun hit Nate full in the face. Wrinkling his nose, he turned to Raziel and realized he wasn't next to him anymore but some meters behind him, leaned against a wall and barely standing.

"Come on," Nate coaxed. "We're nearly there."

He put one of the angel's arms around his shoulders, grabbed his waist, and helped him walk the next two streets. There it was: his home. He opened the door of the house, helping Raziel inside, then silently cursed because he realized they still needed to climb the stairs.

"My apartment's on the second floor. Come, you'll make it."

In the end, he had to practically drag Raziel the rest of the way, but they made it to his apartment. As soon as they were inside, he helped Raziel to his bed, sheets freshly changed after Daniel's visit this morning.

"If you take off the shirt and turn around, I can clean your wounds," Nate suggested.

With hesitation, Raziel slowly turned around. Judging by his stiff movements, he really was in a lot of pain.

"Wait, I also have some pain killers." Nate searched in a drawer and found the small box, then gave Raziel two pills and a glass of water. "Take this and try to relax."

While Raziel took the pain killers, Nate got a bowl with warm water, some cloth, and big sticking plasters to clean the wound. The angel lied down on his stomach, head on Nate's soft pillow, face turned to him, although his eyes were closed.

"Thank you, Nathaniel," Raziel mumbled, before his muscles relaxed.

Had he fallen asleep, or was he unconscious again? And how did he know his name? Nate had never told him. Things just kept getting weirder, but for now, treating these wounds was more important. Carefully, he cleaned all the dirt and blood away. It really looked like remains of wings, burned away. There was even soot around the lesions. What had happened to this guy? And why did he even care? He didn't know Raziel. There was no reason for him to be doing any of this.

He looked at Raziel again for a moment before sighing and leaving him on the bed. His apartment was rather small, with most of it being just one big room. His bed was in one corner, and the other corner contained a sofa. Next to that was his desk, with sketches and notes for songs spread over it. His two guitars were on the wall next to his bed, disregarded and unused lately. It was hard to concentrate on playing, or even composing, when his mind was spiraling.

He should make some food. He hadn't had time for it before Daniel's visit, and Raziel was probably hungry as well. So, he headed into the kitchen. It wasn't really big, but at least it was a separate room. Checking his fridge and cupboard, he decided to just throw some vegetables, pasta, and tofu in a big pan and make something out of that. It should be enough for two people, so Raziel would get some food as well. Not that Nate ate much anyway.

After cooking and eating, he tidied up his apartment a bit and emptied the trash, which mostly contained cigarette butts. It should help to get rid of the stink. Normally, no one was allowed to smoke in his apartment, but Daniel didn't care about that and smoked where and when he wanted to.

Nate pushed that thought aside, taking a deep breath as he grabbed his sketch book and pencil again. Sitting down at his desk, he realized he had to work tomorrow. But how could he go to work when he had a guest he didn't even know? A bit annoyed, he took his phone and texted some coworkers, asking if one of them could cover his shifts the next few days. Maybe he'd get lucky, but he wasn't holding his breath.

The sketchbook lay open in front of him, but he barely noticed it. He was looking at Raziel, instead, who hadn't moved, still lying there as if he was dead already. It wasn't very polite of him to stare, but this guy was fascinating, and he didn't even know why. Junkies were normal; you'd see them every now and then But this one—he was different. Raziel didn't seem like he was on anything, just lost and lonely. Maybe a little weird, too. He reminded Nate of himself, especially after his father had thrown him out.

He tried to concentrate on his sketchbook in front of him, but he honestly had no idea what to draw. Trying to sketch his best friend's cats hadn't ended very nicely last time—drawing animals wasn't easy. And he didn't feel like setting up a still life or anything like that. But maybe...

He sharpened his pencil and started drawing Raziel lying on the bed. Nate wasn't very good yet, but he was practicing and getting better with every single drawing. And something about drawing Raziel felt right. It didn't even look too bad when he was done with it. For a moment, he hesitated before adding wings, two pairs of them, just outlines, for fun. Why did they look so perfect, like they belonged to Raziel?

Then he threw down the sketchbook. What was he even doing? He was staring at his guest again and even drawing him like a stalker. That was so weird. Maybe he should text his best friend to tell him about all this. If anyone could figure out what was going on, it was Jamie. Nate grabbed his phone again to check if someone had offered to take his shifts and was relieved to see he was actually in luck. He'd be free the next two days.

Feeling a little better about the whole situation, he texted Jamie and told him about Raziel. He was the only one Nate could talk to about things like that. It wasn't like he had many friends at all, and Jamie was the only one he could confide in without having to worry he'd be judged. Although they'd only known each other for a few years, they'd become like siblings, always having each other's back, no matter what. Nate also told Jamie what Raziel had explained—that he thought he was a fallen angel. Before he could check the incoming messages, he heard a sound from his bed.

Raziel. He was restless and mumbling, his hands twisting and grabbing onto the sheets. A nightmare? Slowly, Nate sat down next to him and carefully touched his light blonde, long hair.

"It's alright. It's not real," he murmured, hoping that would help. It seemed to work, since Raziel's movements got slower, and he looked up at him with these sad, tired green eyes. "Whatever you were dreaming about, it's not real. It was just a nightmare."

Raziel looked at him silently for a bit, then shook his head. "It wasn't just a dream," he whispered. "It was a memory."

Without further explanation, he sat up a little, brushing his long hair out of his face, and Nate got a better look at his face. He couldn't quite place Raziel's ethnicity. His eyes were green with those beautiful golden sparkles, and his hair was light without dark roots, but the shape of his face and his eyes reminded Nate a lot of one of his favorite Korean singers.

"You should eat something before you rest more," Nate said. "Come on."

He got up and gestured for Raziel to follow him into the kitchen, where he'd left a bowl of food for his guest. Without another world, Raziel sat down and took the bowl, emptying it in just a few minutes. He must have been very hungry.

"You should rest more," Nate told him. "Then tomorrow, we'll talk about everything else, alright? Just..." He grimaced. "My sofa isn't very comfortable, and it's small. We'll have to share the bed. Are you okay with that?"

That was something else Daniel could never hear about, or else he would beat him up—again.

For a moment Raziel thought about it, then he nodded and smiled faintly. "I don't mind."

Slowly, he went back to the bed and laid down. Nate followed him with his gaze for a moment, then felt weird that he was staring again. He grabbed a second blanket from his sofa. It wasn't very thick or warm, but it would do for a night. It was summer, anyway.

He threw the blanket on the bed and took off his jeans but kept the shirt and boxers. He didn't want Raziel to see the scars on his shoulders and back, and he wanted even less to sleep naked next to a stranger. It was bad enough that Raziel could see the other scars littering his body, which he wasn't very proud of.

After turning off the lights, he laid down next to Raziel, grabbed his blanket, and turned to him. "Just one thing," he said. "How did you know my name?"

Raziel smiled at him, turning over as he said, "I told you I was an angel. Good night."

He just stared at Raziel's back. So *that* was his explanation? Maybe he was a stalker. But that didn't make any sense. None of it made sense. These wounds. Raziel appearing out of nowhere. His story. Nothing.

Nate sighed in frustration, turned away from Raziel, and grabbed his pillow. He should sleep and hope this guy next to him wasn't a stalker or murderer. But in the end, what was the worst that could happen?

He didn't care if Raziel killed him. In all honestly, it would be a relief.

CHAPTER THREE

AUGUST 30TH, 2023

When Nate woke up the next morning, he could feel a person's warmth right next to him. Who was this? Their smell was different from Daniel's—not at all like old smoke—and not as tangy as Jamie's. Confused, Nate turned around and slowly remembered the events of the last day when he spotted the person next to him.

Raziel was still asleep and looking so innocent, his hair over his face. He must have turned around in the night, because he was facing Nate now. He was honestly a little surprised to wake up next to the strange man. He'd been half-convinced Raziel was going to kill him in his sleep. But as Nate looked at him, he couldn't imagine the alleged angel harming anyone.

Nate sat on the edge of the bed for a moment, debating what to do. He couldn't do much until Raziel woke up, but he could at least see if Jamie had gotten back to him. So, he got up and headed to the kitchen to grab some water, scrolling through his messages as he went.

According to Jamie's texts, his best friend was just as confused as Nate was, and he was possibly even more curious. When Jamie asked what Raziel looked like, Nate found it hard to describe. He glanced over at his temporary roommate and made sure he was still asleep before taking a picture and sending it to Jamie. It was the easiest way to explain how this guy looked, except the eyes, of course.

Nate relaxed back in his chair and closed his eyes. This whole situation was odd and overwhelming, but at least Jamie would help him understand all this and deal with it. He just wished he had any idea what to do. The only thing he was certain of was that Daniel could never know about this. He'd been relieved this morning to see that his boyfriend hadn't texted yet and asked for another "date."

After another glance at Raziel, Nate decided to make some tea. He didn't like coffee much, so he didn't have a coffee machine. If he wanted a hot drink, it was tea. Maybe he'd make some mint with vanilla and raspberry—his favorite mixture—and put some ice cubes in it. Nate didn't need to drink it hot; he just liked the taste.

Back from the kitchen, he put his mug on the desk and shuddered, the fine hair on his neck standing up, as if he was being watched. As he looked at Raziel again, Nate understood why. The wanna-be-angel hadn't moved, but his eyes were open now, and he was blankly staring at the wall opposite the bed. This guy had cornered the market on creepy.

"Morning," Nate said. "Did you sleep well?"

Raziel's gaze wandered toward him, silently. It was almost eerie and judgmental, but for some reason, it didn't feel uncomfortable, not like it would have if anyone else had looked at him like this—like those green eyes were peering right into Nate's soul.

Without an answer, Raziel sat up and brushed his long hair out of his face, still staring at him. Then he seemed to remember he'd been asked a question. "Yes, sorry, I did. Thank you. Thank you for your help and hospitality. I wouldn't know where else to go."

He'd said that before, but Nate had trouble believing that. Didn't Raziel have *any* friends? Or family? He still wasn't buying the angel story, and he wondered just what this strange man was hiding.

"Yeah, well, it's okay," Nate said, deciding not to push him on it. "If you want to shower, I can give you a towel and a fresh toothbrush as well."

Also, he would need to see if Daniel had left any other clothes here. Even just some underwear would help, though Nate didn't like the thought of this handsome stranger wearing his boyfriend's underwear. But first, Nate took a towel out of a box underneath his bed and searched for a toothbrush in his bathroom. Still freshly packed—perfect. He left both things on the closed lid of the toilet, so Raziel would find them.

When he turned to leave the bathroom, the blonde guy was standing right in front of him, making him jump. *How had he managed to sneak up that close that silently? What was wrong with this guy?*

"Here, go and take a shower, alright?"

He pushed past Raziel, his heart still pounding heavily. This guy would drive him crazy. After a deep breath, Nate searched for fresh underwear for his guest and put it on the bed. Once Raziel was done, he'd go take a shower as well and hope that it helped to calm his nervous thoughts and racing heart. For now, though, he made the bed. Normally, he never did, but having a guest around made him feel compelled to clean up more.

Again, he looked at his phone—five unread messages, all from Jamie. Woah, what was going on with his friend? There was a picture, then a link to an article from yesterday. The last message was "*I'll be at your place in an hour.*" Yeah, great, now things would get even more complicated. Nate sighed and just texted back for Jamie to bring some breakfast, like some toast or whatever. He didn't care much.

By now, Raziel had finished showering, and Nate heard him turn off the faucets. What would Raziel think about Jamie coming over? Why did Nate even care what he thought? And what was so important that Jamie had to come over here to talk about it, anyway? It was all so confusing.

It got even weirder when Raziel left the bathroom—without his towel, completely naked, his clothes clutched in one hand. For a moment, Nate looked at him astonished, then he realized what he was looking at.

"There's fresh underwear on the bed," he said, turning away. "If you need a blow dryer for your hair, it's on the cupboard. I'm gonna go shower."

It all came out in a rush as he skittered around Raziel, trying not to look. His face burned hot, which just made him feel more embarrassed, but he hadn't expected Raziel to just leave the bathroom naked. Who did that when they were a guest in a complete stranger's home?

Safe and alone in his bathroom, Nate took a deep breath, then got undressed and stepped into the shower. The hot water felt good, and it eased some of the tension in his muscles. But he didn't want to take too long in case Jamie showed up, so he quickly rinsed off and stepped back out onto the damp bathmat. As he reached for his towel, he realized he'd made about the same mistake as Raziel. He'd left his clean clothes on the bed. *Great.* Also, his towel was too short to cover both his upper and lower body. He still didn't want Raziel to see his back, the scars littering his skin.

Cursing, he cracked the door open and poked his head through. "Hey, can you give me my clothes? They're on the bed."

Raziel looked confused for a moment, then tossed them to him. With his clothes in hand, Nate closed the door again, put them on, and brushed his teeth. Now he felt better.

For a moment, he looked in the mirror, examining his face. He couldn't be compared to Raziel. He was anything *but* perfect, at least in his opinion—nothing striking about him at all. He had gray-blue eyes that he found rather boring. His hair was cut short, covering his ears and hanging in his face a bit, and it was dyed blue to hide the dirty blonde underneath. He should probably re-dye it soon, actually; it was turning green again, and his roots were showing. He had prominent cheekbones, but nothing else of interest.

Freshly clad and showered, he left the bathroom and spotted Raziel, who was sitting on the bed, legs crossed and without a shirt.

"Ah, right," Nate said. "We should change the plaster on your shoulders."

He grabbed some new ones before sitting down next to Raziel. Careful not to hurt his guest more, he changed the plasters and gave him a fresh shirt.

"My best friend will be coming over soon. Hope that's okay for you?"

Raziel looked at him for a moment, then smiled and nodded. "He will help you understand."

Why was this guy talking in riddles now? Nate wasn't sure if he understood anything right now. It was all just so confusing.

He only watched Raziel, since he wasn't sure what to say or even think. He also didn't dare ask any questions, since anything Raziel said would just lead to more confusion. And besides, Nate probably wouldn't believe any of it anyway.

To do at least something, Nate got up off the bed and sat back down on his chair, where he took his mug and drank some tea, his gaze still on Raziel, who didn't appear fazed at all. He was mostly just looking around the apartment, scanning every item in it.

It felt awkward to just sit there and say nothing, but he didn't know what to say. Nate had never been good at small talk, and Raziel was no exception. He was glad when he heard the doorbell.

Chapter Four

Humanity

AUGUST 30TH, 2023

It must be Jamie.

Finally, Nate's best friend was here, and hopefully, this weird silence would end now. Nate jumped up and pushed the buzzer to open the door downstairs. He waited in the doorway, listening to Jamie's footsteps coming up the stairs. His anxiousness melted a little when his friend reached his apartment and they hugged tight.

"Hey, thanks for coming. And for bringing breakfast!"

Jamie was just amazing. Nate took the food and put it on the small desk next to his sofa, before he turned back to his best friend. Jamie was even shorter than him and rounder. His dark brown hair, which was almost the same color as his eyes and which he had only recently cropped short, was mostly hidden underneath a black beanie hat. Piercings covered not just Jamie's ears but also his face—snakebites and a septum, all glittering silver.

Like most times, Jamie was clad in black jeans, black Doc Martens, and a black bomber jacket, some white and orange cat hair still clinging to the dark fabric. Jamie took off the boots and the jacket, revealing one of his many band shirts, then turned to Raziel, tilting his head curiously. Despite a total stranger popping up in Nate's life, his best friend didn't appear fazed by it. No, instead, Jamie looked curious to get to know Raziel.

"That's Raziel," Nate explained. Then he waved a hand at the man standing next to him. "Raziel, this is my best friend, Jamie."

Raziel's gaze turned toward them, and he smiled. Then he got up, came closer, and held his hand out to Jamie, shaking it. "Nice to meet you. I know you can tell Nathaniel more about me."

What was *that* about? Did Jamie know him? Or was this still about Raziel's delusion that he was an angel.

With a huff, Nate got some plates and knives for their breakfast. Even though the table was small, they should all be able to fit.

"What did you want to show me?" he asked Jamie, while he munched on an un-toasted slice with plum jelly, although he wasn't hungry at all. Nate knew Jamie'd be worried if he didn't eat anything—again. "It sounded pretty important."

Jamie set down the slice of toast he'd been buttering and grabbed his phone out of his pocket. "Right! Here, look at this. It says yesterday afternoon, they spotted some kind of meteor or debris falling from the sky. Here, in Stamdon. No one's found anything yet, and they think it must have broken off before hitting the ground. But it makes sense. If it was Raziel, obviously they couldn't find anything."

"So, you're buying this whole weird story of his?" Nate asked, failing to hide the frustration in his voice.

"Well...I wasn't going to, but..." For a moment, Jamie glanced at Raziel, before he showed Nate the next picture. "I googled the name, and that's what I found. It's supposed to be a portrait of Raziel, an angel. It was drawn centuries ago. But look at it. It could be him."

Nate took the phone and peered at the picture. Jamie was right; it looked a lot like the Raziel sitting next to him—except for the eyes. In this picture, they were as golden as he'd seen them the first time.

Raziel frowned, his nose scrunched up. "Ah, this old one. I don't like it. I look meaner than I am. I like your picture and drawing more."

Nate hadn't realized Raziel had leaned closer to take a peek at the picture, and he startled at the sudden closeness. After he regained his composure, he glared at Raziel, wondering when he'd seen the picture he'd taken yesterday. Had he been reading through Nate's phone like a damn stalker?

"Your phone was on your desk," Raziel explained. "Sorry, but I got curious and wanted to see it."

For a moment, Nate wondered if Raziel could read his mind—and how he'd known the code to unlock the phone. But he also wanted to know why he couldn't be at least a bit angry at his guest. Though he didn't know why, he didn't really mind Raziel looking at his things, his phone even, something not even Jamie was allowed to do.

Nate rubbed his eyes and leaned back, handing Jamie his phone back. "So, if you're really an angel, why did you fall? There must be a reason."

That was how it worked, right? At least, that's what the stories all said. Angels only get banished if they do something wrong, right? It'd been years since Nate had paid any attention to that stuff, but it was still there, swimming around in the back of his mind, even if he no longer believed any of it. But if Raziel was telling the truth, then there was a God, wasn't there? And if that was the case, why did all this terrible shit happen down here on Earth?

"I don't know why I fell, exactly," Raziel said. "My memories are a little distorted. I haven't done anything unrighteous, though; I know that. I'm sure it's Maalik's fault. He envied me, wanted to be just like me. I don't know why." Raziel shook his head. "I lost my home, my family, *everything*. I don't know what I'm supposed to do here. I—" His voice cracked, and he bowed his head.

"Hey. Raziel." Gently, Nate touched the angel's hand, giving him a soft smile when Raziel looked up. "Who cares about why you're here. Let's just try to make the best of it, alright? You can stay with me for now. I'll try to show you more of our world, and hopefully the people upstairs will realize they made a mistake. Even if not, you won't be alone, okay?"

Raziel looked at him astounded, his green eyes dark and watery, but he nodded anyway.

Nate nodded back. "Good. First, we'll go to a secondhand shop and get you some clothes. You can't borrow these forever. You're coming with us?" he asked Jamie, who nodded enthusiastically.

Sure, Jamie was just being nosy. Nate knew his best friend too well—inquisitive to a fault and always up for new experiences. But right now, Nate was glad of it. It meant he wouldn't be alone with Raziel, who still made him nervous.

"Let's go, then."

THE SUN OUTSIDE BARELY reached them because of the buildings all around them throwing shadows, and despite it being August, Nate was a little chilly in only his thin long-sleeved shirt and tight black jeans. He really should've grabbed a jacket or hoodie as well, but it was too late for that.

Whenever he glanced over at Raziel, the angel was looking around, checking out the buildings—all similar gray stone boxes from the 70s with little individuality, every one of them looming four to five stories into the sky. His green eyes were full of wonder, and there was an awed expression on his face. Had the angel ever been on Earth before? Had he ever wandered among humans? Nate wasn't sure if that was even possible for an angel, but if Raziel had, he surely must've seen prettier places than this neighborhood.

"Hey, Raziel, have you ever been here? On Earth?" Nate asked, unsure if the question might be too intimate.

For a moment, Raziel looked at him, before his attention drifted to a teen girl focused on the smartphone in her hands. No, not the *girl*; Raziel's gaze was fixed on the smartphone itself. "Yes, I've been here," he said. "Not long ago, too. But I never had the chance to get to know all this technology."

"We'll teach you about it," Nate promised. "After we've bought some clothes for you."

That was their priority now. Nate didn't like seeing Raziel in Daniel's clothes. It made him feel anxious, like it was wrong somehow. And he also just didn't like being reminded of Daniel, even when he wasn't there.

On their way, they passed a group of teens laughing loudly, a big cloud of smoke over their heads. Nate hated passing groups like this, and he tensed up as they broke into laughter again. How he wished he had his earphones on right now; they made navigating society so much easier. At least they were vaping, not smoking, and the vapor smelled like watermelon or some other sweet fruit, and not at all like Daniel's cigarettes.

Once they passed the group, Nate's tense muscles relaxed a little, and he took a deep breath. A few minutes later, he spotted the neon sign hanging over a store: "*Nifty Thrifty.*" It was a silly name, but the clothes were cheap, and Nate couldn't afford much else.

"Come on. This way."

He gestured for Raziel and Jamie to follow him, and they ended up in the men's section, where Nate searched for some trousers and tops. Jamie was nearby, also looking at different pieces of clothes. Nate wasn't sure if it was for himself or for Raziel, but since Jamie stopped at a rack with a different size, he guessed his best friend wanted to find some clothes for himself.

"Is there anything in particular you want?" Nate asked. "Any colors you like?"

Did Raziel even care about such things? Nate himself didn't like bright colors and preferred black and gray clothes. If Raziel didn't care, he would choose these colors as well—they'd probably look good on the angel anyway.

"I don't care," Raziel replied. "It's gracious enough of you to buy me clothes at all."

Somehow, Nate had expected that answer and just smiled. "Okay! Let's find you something nice."

With Raziel on his heels, Nate searched through racks and racks of clothes of all colors and materials and found some nice pieces here and there, which he hung over his shoulder for now. Nate could only guess Raziel's size—Daniel's clothes fit, but they looked baggy around the shoulders, but at the same time, they were too short for Raziel's height.

At some point, Nate realized Raziel wasn't next to him anymore and found him looking through a different rack, laying shirts over his arm. After some time of collecting a little pile, including some casual shirts, some fancier tops, and several pairs of jeans and pants, Nate turned to his guest. Hopefully they would fit Raziel.

"Here," Nate said, holding the clothes out. "You should try them on so we know if they fit and if you like them."

Without another word, Raziel took the pile, along with the clothes he'd found on his own, and disappeared behind the curtain of the fitting room. Meanwhile, Nate looked around for Jamie, who was walking over with things he'd found.

"You got lucky, too?" Nate asked.

Jamie nodded and smiled, looking a bit embarrassed. "Hopefully it'll fit," Jamie said, then disappeared into the fitting room next to Raziel.

Nate knew it was always a problem for Jamie to find clothes that fit and looked good, but maybe his best friend would really be lucky this time. Most times, they were either too tight or too long for his height. It was a struggle to be short and a bit chubby.

Nate waited outside, hands shoved into the pockets of his jeans, and let his gaze wander around the store, not really taking any of it in. When Raziel pushed back the curtain to show him the first outfit, Nate's attention immediately snapped back to him. He was wearing dark gray jeans and a black shirt, both of which were rather tight. Damn, this guy really was handsome. But he couldn't allow himself to think like that. He barely knew Raziel—and also had a boyfriend.

"Looks good," Nate finally managed after a few false starts. "What do you think?"

Raziel turned around to look in the mirror, brushing his hair to the side to get a better view of the shirt. And it gave Nate a better view of Raziel's backside as well. The jeans certainly accentuated the angel's ass, and Nate noticed faint heat creeping up his face.

"You're right," Raziel said. "It fits me. And it's comfortable."

Raziel looked at him in the mirror, a barely visible smirk on his full lips. Was he flirting? Did he enjoy teasing him? And where would all this get Nate in the end, if he couldn't take his eyes off of Raziel after just a day? Why had he even found this guy? It didn't exactly make his life any easier.

"Then we might take it," he said. "But try the other things as well. We'll decide after that."

It took a lot of effort to say all that without stuttering like an idiot, especially since Raziel's green eyes were still on him. They were mesmerizing, even through the reflection in the mirror, and it was only once Raziel was back in the fitting room that Nate could finally take a deep breath.

He pressed his cool hands to his flushed cheeks, desperate to banish the heat. Nate had no intention of embarrassing himself even more, and while Raziel and Jamie tried on their clothes, he sat down in front of the fitting rooms, waiting for them to show off their choices.

Whenever Raziel presented another shirt, Nate told him his opinion, although it wasn't easy with those tight jeans he kept trying on, which Nate hadn't chosen for him at all. Was this Raziel's taste? The angel must've found them and decided they were perfectly fitting for him—and Nate had to agree. His favorite outfit so far was a pair of black jeans with some rips around the knees and a blood-red dress shirt buttoned only half-way, allowing for a peek at Raziel's chest.

After some time, Jamie was also finished, but put all the things he'd tried on back on the rack. Obviously no luck today, then. Nate felt sorry for his friend, as his life wasn't exactly easy either.

"I need to work out more often," Jamie complained and sat down next to him, his jacket over his knees.

"You're good as you are," Nate insisted. "But I should probably start working out as well."

Nate felt so much like a couch potato, and it sucked. He really wanted to be fitter and feel more confident in his own body, which he hadn't for as long as he could remember.

Jamie's eyebrows creased in concern. "Nate, you're already too thin. First, you need to start eating healthy. Then we can talk about working out."

Nate pouted and looked at the ground. He knew he was too thin, his ribs palpable through his skin whenever he could bring himself to touch himself at all, but he had no idea how to change that. He just couldn't bring himself to eat more.

"Maybe it's a good thing Raziel's here. He has to eat regularly and can help you stick to an eating plan," Jamie suggested, his forefinger tapping against his lower lip.

Maybe Jamie was right, and this really was a good idea. Nate should talk to Raziel about it, although the angel surely had enough other problems.

"I'm wondering what will happen when Daniel finds out Raziel's staying with you?" Jamie asked, leaning a little closer to Nate and whispering so Raziel wouldn't hear their conversation.

Nate hadn't been able to stop worrying about that as well, but what could he do? Daniel always texted before he came over, so he could still send Raziel off for the time. And there was nothing to be jealous about; Raziel was just a friend staying over—not that that would matter much to Daniel.

"I want to break up with him," Nate admitted. "I can't handle this anymore. I want to be happy, and I know Dan will never make me happy."

And now there was Raziel, too, whom Nate found to be quite interesting.

"But you know what will happen if he finds out," Nate mumbled, his heart heavy with the knowledge.

Daniel would beat him and fuck him anyway. Daniel was a jealous asshole who didn't tolerate cheating. He wouldn't even care that Nate hadn't actually cheated; he'd see Raziel living with him as "proof" that he had. On the other hand, it was completely okay for Daniel himself to cheat, as he had done several times already. And every time Nate had sobbed and sobbed, his heart breaking a little bit more. Softly, he touched the scars on his wrist, hidden underneath the fabric of his long sleeves. Even on warm days, he didn't dare wear t-shirts when he went out so that no one could see the scars.

Jamie smiled enthusiastically. "Finally, you've come to your senses!"

His support gave Nate strength. It was the right decision to break up. Daniel had been his anchor for so long, but he was an anchor that dragged him deeper and deeper into darker seas. It was time to let go and explore new areas.

"It's a good decision," Nate heard from somewhere nearby.

Startled, he looked at Raziel. They had been whispering, so how had he heard them?

Again, it was almost like he was reading Nate's mind. "Seems my angelic senses haven't fully disappeared. *Yet.*"

If he was to believe the angel story, it was as good an explanation as any—at least in *this* instance. The only other option was that Raziel was a stalker, but who would want to stalk *him*? Given the two choices, it was honestly easier to believe in angels. Nate realized he'd have to be careful what he said around Raziel. If he could heard and sense more than a regular human, that could lead to trouble.

Raziel, however, seemed unfazed, and simply said, "I've decided what I want to get. Should we go?"

CHAPTER FIVE

New Life

SEPTEMBER 1ST, 2023

It was kind of awkward walking around with Raziel, as Nate basically didn't know this stranger who was crashing at his place. And yet, Nate was comfortable around him, didn't feel threatened or stressed at all. Instead, Raziel was a pleasant guest, not complaining or demanding, despite still clearly being in pain from his wounds.

Since Nate had one more day of free time, he wanted to show Raziel around the city, so he could navigate it more easily on his own. Although he had a phone now—Nate had found an old one in a drawer, and though the battery wasn't the best anymore, the thing still worked—and could check where he was via GPS, Nate didn't want him to get lost or confused. For some inexplicable reason, he cared about Raziel.

"I'll be okay," Raziel promised him, and for a moment, Nate looked at the angel, then focused on their path again, trying to dodge other pedestrians.

"You sure? Your back still looks bad, and it's only been two days."

Two days since the angel's fall, he thought to himself. It wasn't much time to adjust, but despite that, Raziel appeared to be okay. He almost seemed more human than angel, and he was oddly capable of dealing with everything Nate had shown him so far. He'd guessed it would be a lot harder to teach Raziel, show him their ways, but it wasn't at all. It reinforced his suspicions this angel talk was more in Raziel's head than actually true. But then another thought occurred to him: *Did it really matter, though?* Actual angel or mentally ill, Raziel was lost one way or the other.

"It'll heal, over time," Raziel said. "I have to adjust because there's no way back."

A bitter smile curled on Raziel's lips, and for a moment, Nate could see the angel's internal pain, his disbelief at being abandoned like this, being unfairly judged and thrown away. It could very well be a family problem, one that Raziel had convinced himself had religious connotations. Nate had some experience with these, too, and he recognized the look in Raziel's green eyes.

It wasn't right to be discarded like Raziel had been, and he wanted to help him feel better, as much as he could. It sucked feeling so lost and lonely, and he didn't want Raziel to feel like he himself so often did.

Nate couldn't quite communicate these feelings, but he hoped Raziel understood that he cared and was trying to help, that he could be trusted. "Alright," Was all Nate said.

Silently, they walked around, just exploring the city, peeking into some stores, showing Raziel everything he needed to know—like how to buy groceries. It wasn't much, but they got a bottle of lemonade and some cookies to make sure Raziel understood the whole concept of buying and paying for things. After Nate took a sip from the bottle and shared it with Raziel, he put it in his backpack, and they continued on their little walk.

The weather today was annoying, windy and cool despite it being the middle of summer. Nate had had to wear a light jacket if he didn't want to freeze. Whenever a breeze tousled Raziel's long hair, the angel pushed it out of his face again. For a moment, Nate wondered how angels normally looked. Did they all have a human form? Did they all look so ethereal?

"Raziel! Come with me!"

A harsh and commanding voice distracted him from his silly thoughts, and Nate looked around, trying to find the person behind the voice. How did someone know Raziel's name? Nate thought the only other person who knew about him was Jamie, and that definitely wasn't Jamie's voice.

"Kun?" Raziel asked. "What are you doing here?"

Nate followed Raziel's gaze to a stern-looking woman standing a few feet away from them. Her gray suit suggested she was some kind of businesswoman, but the golden irises of her eyes certainly told a different story. They were similar to the golden eyes he'd seen on Raziel just for a moment after he'd fallen.

An angel.

"Come," she said. "I need to talk to you."

Without waiting for their reaction, she strode toward an alley, as if she knew Raziel would follow—which he did without hesitation. It took a moment for Nate to grasp what was going on, and he hurried behind Raziel, following him and the strange angel into the alley, where they could talk more in private.

"Why are you here, Kundaliel?" Raziel asked. "Am I allowed back into Heaven?" Hope and barely contained despair radiated from his voice, reminding all of them he didn't belong here but in Heaven (or *home*?), where he came from. Maybe they had realized their mistake?

Kundaliel exhaled and shook her head, her black curls following the movement. So much for that. She pulled an envelope from her jacket and presented it to Raziel, who hesitantly took it, his hands trembling.

"What's that?" the fallen angel asked with a frown, turning the envelope in his hands.

"Your life, Raziel. Like me, neither Mitzrael nor Phanuel think you're guilty, but it's hard to find evidence. Maalik has a way of swaying the judges, you know him. I don't know if we can bring you back, but we could make your life here easier. Look through it later. Your human will know what it means."

Now it was Nate's turn to frown. Maalik—he had heard that name before. Raziel had mentioned him when they'd talked about why he'd fallen. Maalik was the one who might be responsible for all this. Was there a way to find evidence Raziel wasn't guilty of any of the sins they were accusing him of?

"That's not my human," Raziel said. "That's Nathaniel. He found me, and he's helping me adjust."

Did he actually hear annoyance in Raziel's voice? But why? It wasn't like Kundaliel had insulted him. And even if she had, why would Raziel care? They'd only known each other for a few days.

"Whatever. Make the best of it. If we don't see each other again..." Kundaliel sighed. "It's goodbye, brother."

She glanced at Nate for just a second before ignoring him again and nodding at Raziel. Then she strolled out of the alley, heading who-knows-where and leaving Nate with a *lot* more questions. The most important of which was how did an angel even get on Earth without falling? Then he shook his head, remembering Raziel probably wasn't really an angel. It was possible this woman was part of a cult Raziel had been in, although the golden eyes were rather special and hard to fake, with their faint glow.

"What's in there?" he asked Raziel, careful not to startle him, since the angel appeared deep in thought.

Raziel looked from him back to the envelope in his hands, turning it around, but he didn't open it yet. "Don't know. Can I put it in your backpack until we're back home?"

Nate nodded and took his backpack off to carefully store the envelope in there, knowing this would be a silent and tense walk back home.

"A lesser angel ordering an Archangel around, how pathetic," Raziel mumbled as they went on their way, but Nate didn't dare to ask more questions.

Nate was glad once they were back home, and Raziel could finally open the envelope—if he was actually going to. Right now, the angel was just sitting on the sofa, the envelope in front of him on the table, staring at it as if his gaze alone could explain what was inside.

"Raziel, it's not going to open by itself," Nate carefully reminded the angel.

His words brought Raziel out of his stupor, and he gave Nate a weak smile before leaning forward and grabbing the envelope. He ripped one side open so he could take a look inside, then he frowned and poured the contents on the table.

"The fuck's this?" Raziel said, eyebrow's knitting.

Nate sat down next to him, looking at what he'd received. For him, it was much easier to figure it out, but he still wasn't sure if all this was real. Carefully, Nate took the ID and turned it in his hands, reading it aloud.

"Raziel Park, born August 29th, 1998. Address is the same as mine." He put down the ID and grabbed another paper, a birth certificate declaring Raziel had been born in Chicago, Illinois. Nate also found a social security card and a credit card, all under the same name. Raziel Park. The envelope contained a letter with several notes as well, and he read those out aloud, too.

- *Name: Raziel Park*

- *Parents: Dead*

- *Heritage: Father, American,*

Mother, South-Korean

- *Moved to Stamdon 1 week ago*

- *Memory loss*

Sorry it's so impersonal

"It's your human identity," Nate said. "They made one up for you, so you can legally live here." *Or this is the one Raziel had always had and only forgotten*, Nate added silently.

Nate was stunned by what they held in their hands. Raziel had received a chance for a new life, but it also meant something else.

"There's no way back home," Raziel whispered, the note clutched in his hand, his stare fixated on the words.

Chapter Six

Summons

"You ready?" Nate asked.

No matter how much he wanted to stay at home to have more time to get to know Raziel better, at some point, Nate had to get back to work—and not just because no one could cover his shifts, but because he desperately needed the money as well. Getting paid by the hour was annoying sometimes.

"You're still sure I should come?" Raziel wondered.

He had put on his clothes already, the black jeans Nate liked so much and the blood-red dress shirt. After his long shower, he'd blow-dried his hair, so it was soft and shiny. Nate couldn't deny, the angel looked damn good.

Nate shrugged. "Yeah, it's not like it's any more interesting here. I have to work. Money's not flying in by itself." For a moment, he hesitated, then admitted, almost inaudibly, "And I like your company."

He never should have gotten so involved with Raziel, but what other choice did he have? Was he supposed to have left him on the streets to fend for himself, without knowing a single person? Nate wasn't an asshole.

He sighed and got his backpack, then pushed his wallet and phone into his pockets, leading Raziel out of the apartment and hoping today went well.

When they finally arrived at the cinema where he worked, Nate opened the backdoor and let themselves in. He hadn't been here for almost a week, which was a long time, considering he normally worked five days a week. It was a minimum wage job, but he'd never finished his education, and he didn't really know where to go from here or what to do with his life. There was no energy left in him to search for a better job. Just staying alive drained him enough.

"Nate! You're back," a woman said. "Oh, who's that? Friend of yours?"

A smile lifted on his lips when he heard Lila's voice from the foyer. She was watching him walk down the big marble stairs, with Raziel right behind him. He liked his colleagues; they were nice enough. Very artsy people, but Nate wasn't any different. There was a reason they all liked to work here.

"Yeah, that's Raziel," Nate explained. "He's crashing at my place. Had to show him the city a little."

It was as good a reason as any to have his shifts covered by others. Lots of his coworkers did the same to go party or audition for a movie casting or whatever.

His eyes wandered through the foyer, checking for any differences, but it still looked the same as a week before, as months before, even years and probably decades. Golden wallpaper covered all the walls, and a dark red carpet with black edges filled the floor. Several big armchairs, upholstered in dark brown leather that was cracked at the edges, were placed around smaller tables. The same leather was wrapped around the rim of the bar, some spots patched up with duct tape.

When they headed down the stairs, the bar was to his right displaying glasses and several different bottles of alcohol. To his left was the counter where he would sell tickets, snacks, and sodas. Lots of little jars were stacked in a pyramid shape, containing snacks like chocolate-covered almonds and freeze-dried raspberries. They also sold some regular chocolate bars as well, and, of course, popcorn and nachos.

Nate wandered around the stairs to the office tucked underneath them to clock in and leave his bag in the small beverages lair adjoining the office. Luckily for him, he wasn't tall and didn't hit his head on the low ceiling regularly like some of his coworkers did while refilling their fridges.

When he came back and headed toward his workstation to prepare for customers—heating up the popcorn and turning on all the lights—he noticed Raziel had found a nice spot in one of the armchairs, still watching him.

"Hey Raz, want to watch a movie?" he asked. It took him a second to realize he'd called the angel by a nickname, but it'd felt right, and Raziel didn't seem to object to it either. "Not sure if you'll like any of them, but we got..." He looked at the titles. "...a French comedy or a French drama or...hell, we've only got French stuff at the moment?" he asked Lila, who just shrugged. Typical.

"Normally you like it French, don't you?" she teased as she started the coffee machine and ice machine. "But we also still have *Barbie*."

"Oh, shut up! Not like that!" Nate still had to chuckle. It was good to be back, and most of the time, he could forget his troubles while he was at work, thanks to his coworkers. "What do you think? Comedy, drama, or *Barbie*?"

Raziel flipped through the playbill and read the movie descriptions, then glanced up at Nate with a frown, not looking convinced. That was understandable; most of the movies they showed were made for a different generation, people fifty and over. Except *Barbie*, that is. Their boss had for once understood a movie like that could attract lots of customers, so he'd decided to play that, as well as *Oppenheimer*.

"I guess I'll start easy with *Barbie*," Raziel said. "But I really need to try this popcorn."

Nate just nodded and got one portion ready to go, as well as a Coke. Raziel should have a good time, and their boss didn't really care if they gave free stuff to friends, as long as their work didn't suffer from it, and they didn't overdo it.

"Have fun!" Nate said. "Doors open in, like, fifteen minutes, but I have to work now, so I can't keep you company."

Annoying as it was, like clockwork, their doors opened a quarter of an hour later, the creak of the glass swing doors' hinges announcing the customers strolling in. It was mostly older people, as usual. It was too early for the younger ones to come watch *Barbie*, but Nate actually preferred their older customers over hordes of small children or teens. It was easier to deal with old ladies who were sometimes confused about his dyed hair but were otherwise sweet.

He caught sight of Raziel ducking into one of the theaters, bucket of popcorn in hand, and he hoped the angel would have a good time.

Man, he reminded himself as he handed an older gentleman his change. *Raz isn't an angel.*

But the more he got to know his strange, handsome houseguest, the harder it was to convince himself of that.

SOME HOURS LATER, HE was standing next to Lila at the bar, watching her test a new cocktail she'd created. It certainly looked...*interesting.*

"You sure anyone will want to drink *that*?" he wondered, quite skeptical.

It included egg liquor, coffee liquor, milk, and a splash of vanilla syrup, and it was just a mushy brown. Really weird stuff. But the old ladies who came in *did* like their egg liquor and coffee.

Lila filled a smaller glass for him and pushed it toward him. "Try it. It's not so bad."

Still skeptical, Nate took the glass and stared at the liquid for a moment before taking a sip. Alright, it really wasn't that bad.

"Tastes a little like iced coffee," he said. "But with egg." It was perfect for summer, though, and he took a bigger sip, emptying the small glass.

"See, not bad!" Lila exclaimed. "I wish we could do real daiquiris, too. Y'know, with the whole sugar rim and all."

Nate nodded and rested his chin on his propped-up arm. That would be really cool, but their bar wasn't equipped for or frequented enough to justify learning how to prepare fancier drinks. Still, an easy daiquiri was nice.

"We can still make one for us," he suggested, and Lila immediately grinned and got to work.

It would take some time until their next customers arrived anyway. Movies had just started in all three of their theaters, and Raziel had decided to watch the French comedy after his experience with *Barbie*—a movie Nate had yet to watch.

While Lila was working on the drink, the vibration of Nate's phone and the screen lighting up in front of him announced a new message. He slowly grabbed it to check the messages. Shit, it was Daniel. His relaxed state of mind immediately tumbled into fear and dread, but he had no choice but to see this through.

10pm, your place

will be there

Nate was afraid to see Daniel again, but he had to confront him and finally break up with him. He just had to find somewhere for Raziel to go so he wouldn't be there. If he was, things would get messy, and he really didn't want that.

Nate groaned and grabbed the drink Lila had just finished preparing, hoping a big sip would calm his nerves a little, like it often did.

"Bad news?" she asked.

He just shrugged. His relationship was private, and although many of his coworkers talked about their problems openly, Nate didn't like doing it. He didn't want them to see how weak he actually was and how fucked up his life was.

"It'll be okay," he said. "But I really need this now."

He smiled at her for a moment, then took another sip from his drink. It calmed him down enough that he could think again, and he got an idea: Jamie. Right, he could ask Jamie to pick up Raziel and let him stay at his place tonight.

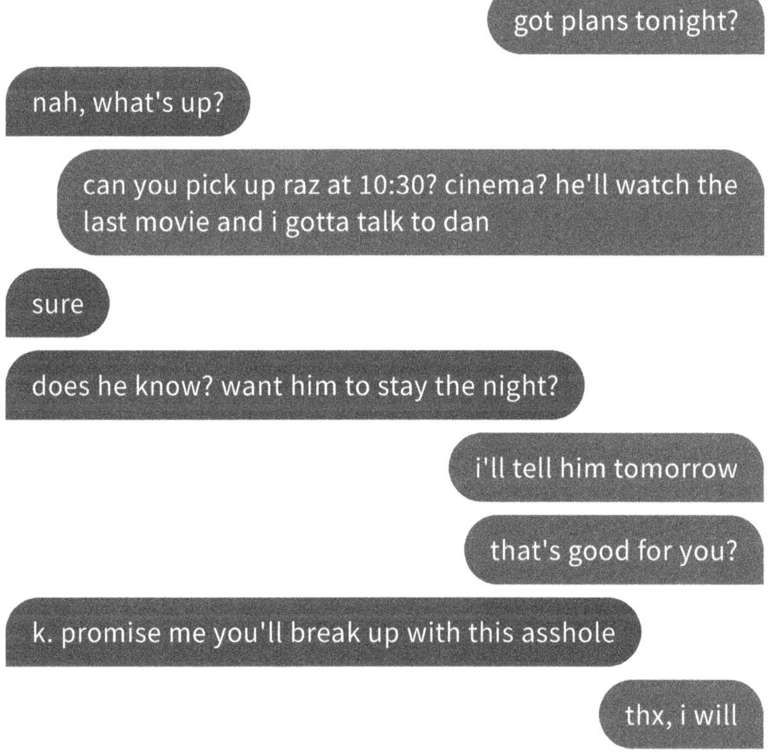

And Nate intended to keep his promise. He was sick of being treated like a pet, like a slave who needed to be available whenever Daniel wanted him, without being loved or cared for.

It wouldn't be easy, though. Whenever he'd tried to break up before, Daniel had persuaded him not to, being all nice and sweet and playing the loving boyfriend for a while afterwards. That is, until he stopped caring and beat him again.

"I think I need another one," he murmured and chugged his drink.

<h1 style="text-align:center">Chapter Seven</h1>

<h1 style="text-align:center">Scars</h1>

SEPTEMBER 3RD, 2023

Nate had yet another drink before he headed home. Raziel was watching another movie, so he didn't say goodbye. Jamie could fill him in when he picked him up later. Nate had to do this alone, despite how afraid he was of Daniel's reaction.

When he arrived home, he could see his boyfriend sitting on the doorstep. Like every time, Daniel was wearing dark cargo pants, formerly white sneakers yellowed by use, a baseball cap to hide his messy dark hair, and a dark gray shirt that allowed for a peek of the sleeve tattoo on his left arm. It was badly inked and blurred, with some raised lines. There were deep lines between Daniel's eyebrows, and his mouth was pressed into a thin line. Shit, he was already angry. This wouldn't be a good evening.

"You're late." Daniel got up and stared down at him. "And you're drunk."

Nate just shrugged and said nothing. Daniel wasn't wrong; he was a little drunk, but he wouldn't be able to deal with this otherwise, wouldn't have the courage to have this talk with Daniel. He never had. Instead, he just ducked and endured.

Nate unlocked the door to the house and noticed Daniel's heavy footsteps behind him. They made the hair on his neck stand up and followed him to his apartment door and inside, where he locked it behind them and turned to face Daniel.

"Daniel, I—"

Before he could say more, he was grabbed by the throat and kissed violently, tasting and smelling the smoke on Daniel's lips. His piercing pressed cold against Nate's own lips, and his badly trimmed beard scratched Nate's chin. It sent a shiver of fear through him, the knowledge of what was inevitably to come.

Daniel pushed him to the couch, where he was pressed down into the pillows.

"Daniel, wait, I—"

"Shut the fuck up," Daniel grumbled, his fingers firmly anchored in Nate's blue hair.

Daniel wouldn't listen; he never did. No matter what Nate wanted to say, he would be told to shut up, told to... He shivered again, feeling nauseous. But he tried to relax, to let the alcohol take over his body and mind, to forget what was going on while Daniel tore his shirt off of him and opened his own pants.

"Suck my dick, bitch," Daniel commanded, dragging Nate to his crotch and not giving him a choice in the matter.

It was like every other time. Daniel did whatever he wanted, used him, pushed him around until they ended up on the bed, Nate's face pressed into the pillow, where he tried to gasp for air whenever Daniel allowed him to move.

When they first started sleeping together, the sex had been good. Daniel had taken care of him, made him feel wanted and loved, but it had soon turned to shit. Nothing Daniel did felt good, and Nate wasn't quite paying attention to what he was doing anymore. He had learned to ignore the pain and let his mind wander into a different reality, disassociate from what was happening to his body. If only he could stay in his imaginary universe forever, but Daniel's hollering pulled him out of his peaceful fantasies.

"The fuck's this? That's not mine!"

Nate froze when Daniel grabbed the shirt on the floor next to the bed. *Raziel's* shirt.

"This your tranny friend's stuff?" Daniel demanded. "Or are you getting fucked by other dicks?"

Daniel dragged and pushed him around until Nate was on his back, staring up at his boyfriend, who was looming over him, anger and disgust in his dark brown eyes. Why had he even dealt with him for so long? Whatever he said, it wouldn't change things. Daniel would think and believe what he wanted to, no matter what Nate said.

"It's a friend's, and he's not a tranny." Using that word made him feel even sicker, but Nate would protect Jamie, no matter what. "And I've never cheated on you." Not like Daniel had so often. For a moment, he hesitated, wondering if he could really do this. Then he said, "I want to break up."

This was probably the worst possible moment to say that, but he'd gotten it out. And, really, how much worse could things get? What else could Daniel do to him that he normally didn't?

But a second later he knew, his cheeks burning hot from where he'd been struck, then Daniel's hand was tight around his neck, cutting off his airflow and pressing him into the mattress with his full weight.

"You fucking bitch!" Daniel screamed. "You think you could do better?! You're mine, and you better not forget that!"

Nate barely felt Daniel fucking him again; he was too occupied with trying not to pass out and struggling against the strong grip around his neck. No matter what he did, Daniel had him pinned down well, and even Nate's fingernails scratching his arms didn't make a difference; neither did the helpless flailing of his legs. Nate's body became more and more limp, and black specks clouded his sight.

Daniel would kill him, right here and now. Suffocate him. How funny. He'd always guessed he would end his own life.

Suddenly, oxygen rushed into his lungs. It burned and made him cough. As Nate turned on his side, his body was convulsing with the sudden rush of air in his lungs. Daniel just snorted behind his back, then a hard smack on his ass made Nate wince.

He kept lying on his side, still gasping while his body slowly recovered. The familiar click of a lighter sounded in his ears, and his body instinctively curled up more. He started shivering, and soon the typical stink of Daniel's cigarettes burned in his nose.

The mattress beside him shifted as Daniel sat down behind him again, almost gently caressing his upper arm.

"You remember now whose bitch you are? Don't you dare trying to break up with me or fuck with others. If you try this shit again, I'll kill your lover and then *you.*"

Daniel leaned closer, and soon, heat and pain burned into Nate's shoulder. A low whine escaped his sore throat at the so-familiar feeling of a lit cigarette being put out on his bare skin, leaving yet another scar on his back. But Daniel's hand firmly closed around his upper arm, holding him still.

Another click to re-ignite the cigarette followed, and Daniel took a drag from it before putting it out again, leaving more marks on his skin. And again. *And again.* All over his shoulder and back, until the last mark found its way on his ass. Nate cried in pain and choked on the spit and bile rising up his throat, while he tried to escape the torture, but Daniel stopped him, his hand gripping his waist, surely leaving bruises there as well.

"Hey, hey, don't, babe. I have to show you you're mine, hm? Like your daddy always did." Daniel's fingers traced the dozens and dozens of scars on his back and shoulders that he'd collected during his life. "So you'll never forget me." The kiss on his shoulder, right next to a new wound, made him shudder in disgust and fear.

The mattress shifted again when Daniel got up, and the rustling of clothes was a relief. It meant Daniel was getting dressed and would leave in a moment. One last slap on his ass made Nate quiver, but not once did he look at...his boyfriend. Still.

"See you soon, babe."

He could hear the grin in Daniel's voice and was so glad when the door of his apartment closed again.

Nate wasn't sure how long he just lay there on his still-soiled bed, unable to do anything but stare at the wall and feeling just as filthy and used as his sheets. His whole body hurt, and his throat was sore, as was his ass. The burn marks still smarted, and the stench of cigarette butts filled Nate's nose, making him nauseous.

Why?

Why was it always him? What had he done in life to deserve such treatment? Had he angered God and was receiving punishment? Or was he just an unlucky bastard, fucked by life over and over again?

Slowly, he dragged his aching body out of bed, scuffled to his little kitchen, and grabbed the bottle of Jägermeister right from the fridge. He took the first sip while he made his way to the bathroom. The alcohol burned in his mouth and throat, but it was a soothing sensation as well, cool in his mangled esophagus.

He lurched into the shower, and when hot water finally splashed down on him, Nate was at least a little relieved. No longer was he drenched in traces of Daniel. The new wounds burned every time they were hit by the water, but he didn't care. The alcohol would numb his pain soon enough.

Slowly, he slid down the wall, kneeling on the shower floor. Nate was sick, nauseous, and his head was spinning. It was all wrong. So *wrong*.

He couldn't stop his body from emptying the contents of his stomach, puking it all up. It was basically just the alcohol he'd drunk today because he hadn't eaten much again, just some cereal in the morning. Now, not just his windpipe burned, but his whole throat did, and a dry laugh escaped his lips, which turned into a coughing sob soon enough.

The traces of his hurling were washed away, and he tilted his head to drink some hot water directly from the stream of the shower. Then he grabbed his bottle again and took a few more swigs. He didn't want to be sober. Not now. He didn't want to think or feel; he just wanted it all to be over. All the pain, the memories of tonight and so many nights before, were replaying endlessly in his head, and Nate just wanted it to *stop*.

He stayed in the shower for a long time, enjoying the hot water while his bottle got emptier with every sip. But once his head started swimming and the hot water turned cold, he had to admit it was time to get out of the shower.

Lazily, he wrapped himself in a towel and stumbled through his apartment until he fell onto his sofa. Nate couldn't sleep on the bed, not while it was still soiled from Daniel. Instead, he pulled the blanket over his body, set the bottle next to him on the small table, and tried to sleep.

Hopefully the nightmares would stay far away tonight.

His life was enough of a nightmare already.

CHAPTER EIGHT

Pride

SEPTEMBER 4TH, 2023

Nate woke up when he heard the key in the lock of his apartment door. With a still mushy brain and a pounding headache, he remembered what'd happened. Daniel had visited him last night, and Nate had gotten hammered afterward. He was still a little drunk and so damn tired.

Slowly, he turned around to face the door and see who entered. No one had a key to his apartment except...*Raziel*. Nate cursed, suddenly a lot more awake and agitated, since he certainly didn't want the angel to see him like this. Raz couldn't know how pathetic he was, how he was unable to protect himself from his own boyfriend.

"Don't you dare come in here!" he yelled.

Nate at least wanted to put on clothes and hide his scars, but instead, his blanket tangled around his legs, and he crashed onto the floor next to the couch. Despite his efforts to keep Raziel out, the door still opened.

"Nate?"

Of course, the angel didn't listen.

Why did no one listen to him when he asked for something? Daniel didn't, and now Raziel didn't either. Nate picked himself up from the hard wooden floor and tried to untangle the blanket as quickly as possible so he could wrap it back around himself. Every movement hurt, from his pounding head to his sore throat and throbbing back, down to his trembling legs.

Raziel's piercing gaze was upon him as soon as the door clicked shut, but Nate didn't dare look at him. Instead, he tried to rush into his bathroom as fast as possible. That wouldn't do him any good either because there were no fresh clothes there. But he could hide until Raziel got bored of him and left, just like everyone else in his life did once they were bored of playing with him. His heart pounded painfully against his chest, panic at the idea of getting left on his own again mixing with memories of the night before.

"Nate, what happened?"

He heard Raziel's voice and his steps approaching, until his body came into view, blocking his way. Raziel was much faster than Nate in his beat-up state. He should've known there'd be no escaping the angel. Great. Why had Nate taken in this guy? Why had he given him a spare key? He'd been such an idiot to do so.

"My life's a fucking mess, that's what happened," Nate said.

He tried to push Raziel aside, but the angel stood like a pillar in front of the bathroom door, unmoving. Nate wasn't looking at him, but he could sense his gaze, and he imagined it was full of pity. That's what Nate was. Pitiful. Not even Jamie knew the full extent of his relationship problems or about his scars, so there was no way he was going to tell a literal stranger about them.

"It's okay Nate," Raz said soothingly. "You don't have to do this on your own."

Not on his own, sure.

Warm, soft hands gently gripped his shoulders, making Nate wince as pressure was applied to one of the burns. There was so much fear inside him, even though it wasn't Daniel in front of him, even though Raziel smelled like cedar wood—just like Jamie.

Nate growled and pushed Raziel with more force this time, a desperate attempt to get away from him. He was relieved when the hands disappeared, but it had the unfortunate side effect of tugging on the blanket, which started slipping away. His drunk lack of coordination didn't do him any favors, either, and the blanket slid off his shoulders, revealing naked skin and some of his marks—fresh and old.

A warm hand cupped his chin and nudged it up, urging him to look at Raziel. Nate realized it wasn't pity in the angel's eyes; he was staring at his neck, then his gaze wandered toward his shoulder.

"Who did this to you?" the angel asked, his voice soft and laden with worry.

Nate couldn't believe he actually cared. Why should Raz care about him?

"Get the *fuck out!*" Nate screamed.

His throat burned, and he coughed as he stumbled backward, away from the gaze and the hand, away from all the comfort and protection Raziel might give him. He didn't want it, didn't want any pity. He didn't need a savior, a *guardian angel.* It was absurd. He didn't deserve such a luxury—both his father and Daniel had beaten that into him. He deserved *nothing.*

But there was no escape. Raziel took two big steps toward him, bridging the distance, and pulled him into his arms. They were strong, warm, and held him close, pressed against the angel's chest.

It was so good.

No matter how much Nate despised appearing weak before others, being held like this was heavenly. Maybe, just maybe, he could lean into this, just for a moment. Raziel was no human, and he wouldn't be here forever. But he could be an anchor, could be his distraction. At least that's what Nate wanted to believe right now—that he deserved a guardian angel, that he wasn't alone anymore.

Tears filled his eyes, desperate to escape and release some of the pressure Nate held inside himself, but he forced them back as he relaxed against the angel's chest and leaned into the hug. He grabbed Raziel's shirt with one hand and leaned his head against his shoulder. Raz smelled so good, so fresh, and not at all like cold smoke, as Daniel always did, but like Jamie's shower gel—cedar wood and citrus.

"It's okay, you can relax with me," Raziel whispered, his cheek leaned against Nate's hair, and a silent sob escaped Nate.

Could he really relax with Raz? He wanted to so desperately. He was tired of being alone, of dreading waking up on his own every single day, of dragging himself through another loveless, cold day. But since he had found Raz, he hadn't felt as lonely and lost as he had in the months and years before.

The warm hand on his cheek nudged him to look up again, and Raz brushed away some of his tears, which had managed to escape despite Nate's struggle to keep them at bay. A sweet, loving smile was on Raz's full lips, and with a shivering lower lip, Nate managed to put on a tiny smile as well.

"You're ice-cold," Raziel said. "Come, I'll make you some tea, you put on some clothes, and then you rest some more."

Only once Raz mentioned it did Nate realize he was shivering despite clinging to the blanket and Raziel's warmth. The alcohol in his blood still clouded his feelings, made his brain sluggish and his body slower to react to his environment.

He didn't fight Raziel guiding him back to the sofa, just silently sat down. His attention was still on Raz as the angel grabbed his sweatpants and a shirt. Even as Raz handed him the clothes, Nate didn't move from the sofa to change into them yet. Instead, he stared at Raziel, who grabbed the bottle of booze on the table and sniffed it. With a frown on his face, he took it back to the kitchen.

"Please put on clothes," Raz reminded him.

Slowly, Nate let the blanket slide down. His upper body was fully revealed now, but he quickly put on the shirt. Raziel might have seen some of the scars on his shoulder, but there was no reason to let him see all of them.

The fresh wounds hurt when the fabric brushed against them, and so did his neck, waist, and ass. It wasn't comfortable to sit at all, so Nate laid down on the sofa and curled up with a pillow in his arms. Hoping to distract himself from what'd happened, he turned on the TV to watch some dumb show. He didn't care what was on and ended up watching a cartoon while Raziel was doing whatever in the kitchen. Nate could hear clinking, then his fridge falling shut again.

It was pathetic. Now he really had a guardian angel. Only he didn't let Raziel protect him when it was important. No, his angel only saw the aftermath of how fucked up his decisions and life were.

When he felt a breeze, his gaze wandered around the apartment again. Raziel hadn't just put a big cup of steaming tea in front of him; he'd also changed the bed sheets, emptied the ash tray, and opened a window. Fresh, cool morning air filled the apartment, making him shiver again, but at least the smell of smoke and bad sex slowly disappeared.

"Drink some tea," Raz said. "It'll warm you up. Did you eat today? Or yesterday?"

There was worry in Raziel's voice and expression, but Nate still couldn't really believe it. Raz hadn't given him a reason to distrust him, and yet Nate didn't dare believe in anything good happening to him, no matter how concerned Raz looked.

Slowly, Nate pushed himself into a sitting position to grab the tea and take a sip, immediately burning his lips and tongue. Fuck, way too hot still. Instead of answering verbally, he just shook his head. He hadn't eaten, and he doubted he could manage to force down any food now. He was still nauseous.

By now, Raziel knew him a little better, knew that he didn't eat much. Hopefully he wouldn't try to force him to eat more, but Nate knew his hope was in vain. Of course, Raziel would make some food. Or try to make some. He didn't think cooking was something angels knew how to do. When Raziel came back from the kitchen, though, Nate sighed in relief. He hadn't tried cooking and was simply holding a bowl of cereal and a glass of water, to soothe the burning the too-hot tea had inflicted.

"Eat, please," Raz pleaded as he sat down next to him.

Nate noticed the golden sparkles in his green eyes shined more today. Or maybe it was just an illusion, the sun and his hungover mind playing tricks on him.

Hesitantly, Nate took the bowl and ate some spoonfuls until it was half-empty. He already felt sick again and opted to drink some water rather than finish his food.

"Do you want to talk about what happened?" Raziel offered.

Nate glanced at him for a moment, then shook his head again, clinging to his mug to drink more tea. The warmth helped him relax, but it also drowned out the numbing effect from the alcohol. Very slowly, his brain started working again.

Shit, he had to work today.

"Where's my phone?" he wondered, his voice a little raspy.

Raziel got up and grabbed the phone from the nightstand, then handed it to Nate before sitting down next to him again.

There were some messages from Jamie, but otherwise, there wasn't much else going on. And then he saw it—he had a message from Daniel.

Bile rose in his throat at the message, but Nate fought to keep his small breakfast down. He didn't want to see Daniel ever again, but of course he knew it was hopeless. He'd tried breaking up and where had it gotten him? Nowhere. It was better if he just played nice, relaxed, and spread his legs when Daniel visited him. It was easier than resisting. Whenever he'd tried that, he just got hurt even more.

His eyes were still burning as he swiped away the message and checked the clock. 12:31pm. Shit, he had to get dressed for work.

"Gotta get to work soon," he informed Raziel and got up, still swaying a little, to search for fresh clothes in his closet, at least fresh underwear, socks, and shirt. He didn't care about his pants. He didn't have many pairs anyway.

"I'll come with you," Raz decided. "But this time I won't let you put me in a seat to watch weird movies."

"Like I forced you," Nate scoffed.

"You're right. Still, I prefer hanging out in the foyer with you."

Raziel smiled at him softly and with such an honest expression, Nate had to believe he really meant what he said.

Not knowing how to respond, he went into the bathroom to change and to let Raz get dressed in the bedroom. Brushing his teeth also sounded like a nice idea, and as he reached for his toothbrush, he caught sight of himself in the mirror. Now he knew why Raziel had been staring at his neck. Bruises covered his light skin, some more distinct than others. No wonder his throat hurt so much.

He huffed and combed his hair, not that it made much of a difference, before he headed out the bathroom.

Another day of work.

CHAPTER NINE

Halcyon

SEPTEMBER 15TH, 2023

A day just for Jamie and Nate. They hadn't had that for a long time, not with everything going on and their shifts colliding so often. Raziel, who'd gotten a job at the cinema a week or so earlier, had taken over his shift for today, so Nate could spend time with his best friend. They both needed this time together, and he was thankful to have the opportunity.

"It's a little weird that an angel has a job selling popcorn and movie tickets," Nate mused as he leaned back on Jamie's bed.

"A little," Jamie agreed. "It's weird he's got a whole human identity at all, but it helps a lot. It'd get really expensive to feed him on your own."

Jamie wasn't wrong. Nate didn't make much money at his job, barely enough to support himself, so it was good to have Raziel making his own money and paying for part of the groceries and rent. Nate still wasn't entirely convinced Raziel was actually an angel, but he didn't care much anymore. Whatever Raziel had gone through, it had been bad, and Nate was in no place to deny his new friend his reality.

"Your roommate's not home?" Nate wondered.

Alex didn't really like when Jamie had visitors over—not that Jamie did that often. It was basically just Nate, and that had been rare lately as well. From what Nate had gathered, Alex and Jamie had been fighting a lot lately, and he felt sorry he hadn't been there more for Jamie. It reminded Nate of what a bad friend he was, one who wasn't even capable of supporting his own best friend, who had become like a brother for him—one he actually loved and cared for.

Jamie sighed deeply and got up from his bed, stretching his arms before he deflated again. A tired smile was on his lips, and Nate wondered what exactly had been going on lately. They hadn't talked much about Jamie's struggles, his life; when they'd talked these last few weeks, it was mostly about Raziel and Daniel.

"Nah, she's working tonight," Jamie said. "She wants to move out and is searching for her own place. I should, too, but you know how it is, finding affordable places."

Jamie shrugged and shot him a crooked smile. Of course, Nate knew the struggle. Affordable apartments were rare, and sometimes hundreds of people applied for one single shitty apartment. It had been pure luck he had found his own.

"Or..." Jamie stopped and glanced at him, struggle clear in his voice.

"Or what?" Nate wondered, leaning forward on the bed despite sitting cross-legged. He wanted to show Jamie he still cared and was still his friend. Nate couldn't afford to lose the only anchor he had in his life.

"You could move in?" Jamie mumbled, almost inaudibly. "I mean, it'd be cheaper for both of us, and I love spending time with you. Raziel's included, of course."

Nate noticed how nervous Jamie was proposing this option, shifting from one leg to the other. It wasn't a bad idea, and it would certainly save them both money. And, of course, Nate liked spending time with Jamie as well, but he also wouldn't have his own space anymore, no place where he could hide when his bad days hit him hardest. Not that he really had his home to himself anymore with Raziel being there most of the time. Would it be such a big change?

Change was never easy for Nate, and it would be a big change to move in with his best friend, give up the small apartment he called his own. He'd have to share a room with Raziel for real, but there was also the kitchen and living room to escape to more easily.

He honestly couldn't decide right now. He had to weigh the pros and cons, and there was Raziel to think about, too. Would the angel want to move in here? Would he be okay sharing a room with Nate even though they weren't a couple? Hell, did Nate want to do that either? He wasn't sure, though he couldn't deny that it was an intriguing prospect, one that warmed his heart in a way he'd rarely experienced before.

"I'll think about it, alright?" he said.

"Sure. I'll get us drinks, and you choose the movie today," Jamie said and left the room.

Glad for the distraction, Nate grabbed the PlayStation controller and started the console to search around on Netflix, until he settled on a movie. *Snowpiercer*. It was a little weird, but he liked the movie nonetheless.

Soon, Jamie was back with two glasses filled with a dark brown liquid. Nate didn't really care what it was, just took the glasses and put them on the nightstand. Jamie turned his back to him to take off his shirt and his binder before he put his shirt back on, a purple one, already littered with white cat hair.

"Now I'm ready for a good movie! What'd you chose?" Jamie asked, planting himself next to Nate on the bed and leaning against the wall with his legs crossed. Before Nate could answer, Jamie spotted the title and nodded in agreement. "Ah, we've seen this one already, right? Perfect!"

Nate smiled and hummed in agreement as he took his glass and pressed play. It was always good to watch movies they already knew, since they could talk more then. When he took a sip from his glass, he realized Jamie had made them whiskey-cokes, and he relaxed back.

Soon, Nate perceived a warm, fuzzy presence next to him and spotted a brown-white tabby cat next to him, purring and asking for attention. He petted the small animal, scratching her chin and behind her ears.

"She loved Raziel, by the way," Jamie said, nodding at the cat. "What's going on between you two, anyway?"

Jamie turned toward him more, and immediately, Nate felt insecure and nervous, his heart beating faster when he thought of Raziel. Well, what *was* going on between them? Good question. He wasn't even sure. He knew Raziel was a good guy and took care of him, especially after Daniel's last visit, but there was so much broken trust in Nate. How could he allow people in his heart again, when it just got broken over and over? He was already an empty shell—at some point, nothing of him would be left anymore.

"He's pretty and all," Nate admitted, "but...I don't know. I still haven't broken up with Daniel."

The thought made Nate even more insecure, since he knew very well Daniel could text him any day now to ask for another "date." Just thinking about it made his heart tighten as nausea hit his stomach. It had been almost two weeks since Daniel's last visit—an uncommonly long time. Instead of being glad about it, the silence put Nate on edge. No matter how afraid he was of Daniel, no matter how much he wanted to break up with him, Daniel was still his boyfriend, the only person who had shown him any kind of love for so long.

Jamie's voice cut through his thoughts. "Nah, that's not true. You *did* break up with him. Doesn't matter what he says about it. It's not a divorce where both parties have to sign. You're done. And Raz is much hotter anyway."

Logically, Nate knew that was true, and yet there were so many doubts inside his heart and mind. So many thoughts dragged him down, too many to speak them aloud. Nate was afraid that if he gave voice to them, they'd become even more true than just in his head. And yet, Jamie deserved the truth.

"I've only known him for what, not even three weeks now?" Nate said. "Also, he's way too hot for me. Too good and caring. I don't deserve his love. Doubt he's even interested in a fuck-up like me."

There, he'd said it. He didn't think he deserved Raziel, not in any way. Being around him was already wonderful, and since Raziel knew so much about him, it made him vulnerable. And Nate didn't like being so vulnerable.

"Nate, hey, look at me." Jamie grabbed his hand and waited until Nate finally returned his gaze. "You deserve the best in the world, alright? It's not my place to say Raz is right for you, but you deserve love. A caring boyfriend. Someone you can trust."

If Jamie only knew how much Raz already knew about him, things he had never told or shown his best friend, things he had always hidden, always covered up. It wasn't fair to Jamie, he knew that; his best friend trusted him with all his problems and worries while Nate closed himself up regularly. Still, Nate couldn't bring himself to tell Jamie how Daniel treated him or how Nate treated *himself*. How hurt and broken he actually was inside.

"I..." What? What should he say? He didn't know. His throat closed up, and Nate squeezed his eyes shut, forcing back the tears. Then he leaned forward, his forehead against Jamie's shoulder. "Thanks. For being there for me...even when I'm an idiot."

Jamie chuckled and patted his back. "Don't worry. You support me all the time, too. And I'll support you, no matter if you want to try things with Raziel or not. Whatever happens, I'm here for you, and you won't get rid of me. That's a threat!"

Nate had to smile, glad his best friend had managed to cheer him up a little, even if just for the moment. Although Jamie still didn't know about everything that was going on, Nate felt reassured that he wouldn't be alone, no matter what happened next.

"Oh, just one thing," Jamie said. "Gimme your phone."

A bit confused, Nate looked up and spotted Jamie's outstretched hand, awaiting his phone. Reluctantly, Nate pulled it from his pocket, but kept it in his hand still. "What are you planning?" he asked uncertainly.

"I'm getting rid of one of your problems," Jamie said, a cheeky grin on his lips and a mischievous sparkle in his eyes.

Nate still wasn't sure about this, but he trusted Jamie, so finally, he handed him his phone. Nate tried to lean closer to see what Jamie was doing, but his friend kept the phone out of his sight. After a few minutes, Jamie gave him his phone back, but Nate couldn't spot any differences at first glance.

"Jamie? What did you do?"

"Oh, just deleted and blocked a certain asshole because you *still didn't do that*. Fuck him, he never deserved you."

Jamie beamed at him, and for a moment, Nate was completely stunned. Jamie had blocked and deleted Daniel's number? He didn't even know what to say. The knowledge that Daniel couldn't just text and command him anymore was a relief, but Daniel still knew where he lived and could show up any time. Jamie had no idea how aggressive Daniel could get when he didn't get what he wanted, and rising anxiety mixed with his relief.

Nate had the feeling this wasn't over yet, but he decided not to say anything. Instead, he sat back up to try and watch the rest of the movie. It wasn't a bad one, but Nate couldn't really pay attention this time. He had a lot of things to think about, aside from Daniel. Did he want to try things with Raziel? Did angels even pursue relationships? And if they did, was Raziel interested in *him*? He could only find out if he was ever brave enough to ask.

"Oh, I wanted to show you something!" Jamie proclaimed excitedly as soon as the movie had ended.

He swapped to the YouTube app and searched for a music video. Nate had heard the band's name, but he couldn't remember where. Rather than thinking about it, Nate chugged the rest of his drink and put the glass down on the nightstand.

"Here, have you seen them?" Jamie asked. "That's Hizumi's new band. I love their vibe!"

Hizumi? Shit, really? He loved this guy. How had he missed this? The video was already two years old, but it was damn cool. Hizumi's voice gave Nate goose bumps immediately, just like every time, and he couldn't help but stare at the screen.

"Fuck, he's still hot. And his voice..." Nate swooned, mesmerized by the singer performing to the music.

Jamie chuckled and he relaxed on his stomach, looking up at Nate. "Yeah, you always had a thing for Asian guys. Raz should be right up your alley then."

Playfully, Nate shoved his best friend. Jamie was only teasing. Nate had had a few crushed on some J-Rock musicians before, but looks weren't really all that important to him. Though, that didn't stop him from thinking Raziel was cute. And caring. And badass. He was too good for Nate and it scared him how much he cared about the angel—and how much Raziel cared for *him*.

"Oh, also, we should go to a concert again, don't you think?" Jamie said.

Now it was Nate who chuckled since it was just so typical of Jamie to change topics like this. But that's just how he was, and Nate loved that about him. It was also a good thing Jamie dragged him to some social things from time to time, otherwise, he'd never go anywhere.

"Sure, tell me when someone interesting is around," Nate said.

How long had it been since the last concert? Surely several years—probably before the first lockdown. He could really use the distraction, and he missed spending time with Jamie

Nate fell on his back and stared at the ceiling. It was a good day today, and he shouldn't worry about anything. The alcohol helped him to relax more, to push aside thoughts of Daniel and Raziel. Nate really had needed this evening with Jamie, and he knew he could stay the night without worrying about how to get back home. A fluffy orange cat cuddled against his side and started licking his hand while she purred at him, and Nate was okay.

These were the good days, and he had to cherish every single one of them. They were too rare and precious.

Chapter Ten

SEPTEMBER 29TH, 2023

"You free tomorrow?" Jamie wondered, watching Nate clean out the popcorn machine for the next day. He'd stopped by toward the end of Nate's shift.

"I think so, yeah. Shouldn't have a shift. Let me check." Nate finished what he was doing and pulled out his phone to check his schedule. "Yup, I'm free. Why, what's up?"

Jamie shuffled around nervously and scratched his cheek, a sign whatever he had planned was important. "I've got an appointment at Planned Parenthood at 6pm," he finally spat out. "Could you maybe come with me? I'm just really nervous and scared."

Surprised, Nate looked up, then gave him a bright smile. He knew how much Jamie had been wanting to get on T; he'd been trying to get an appointment since he'd come out several months ago.

"Of course! If you want me there, I'll be there," Nate promised.

It was hard for Nate to imagine how Jamie must feel, his body and gender not aligning the way he wanted them to. Now that his friend was finally going to take the first step into medically transitioning, hopefully it would make things easier for him, give him the confidence and comfort he deserved.

"Thanks!" Jamie beamed at him. "Oh, if Raz wants, he can come, too. Then we can go to a club after the appointment and celebrate."

It was an interesting proposition. As far as Nate knew, Raziel had never been to a club before, and he wasn't even sure if the angel would enjoy himself. But he liked the thought of spending time with the two guys he cared about most, especially on such a special day.

As the angel wandered over, carrying a beverage crate, Nate asked, "Raz, want to come with us tomorrow? Jamie got an appointment, and we want to go party at a club afterward."

Raz put the beverage crate next to the fridge, and pushed his long hair back. Nate's heartbeat picked up a little. They still hadn't talked about what they expected from each other, but one thing was clear: Nate was very attracted to this handsome angel.

There was no hesitation in Raziel's answer. "Sure! I've always been curious about clubs. Nik and Dylan keep inviting me to come with them, but I've been nervous."

Nate wasn't surprised that their coworkers had invited him out considering they loved to party, coming into work still hungover and with about three hours of sleep. But it was fine, they still got the job done, and Nate wasn't any better. In fact, he wondered if maybe he was worse, drinking at home by himself rather than out with friends

"Cool, then we'll do that tomorrow," Jamie said with a beaming smile that turned soft a moment later. "Thanks, Nate."

Nate smiled back. "Of course! What are friends for?"

SEPTEMBER 30TH, 2023

On their way to the clinic, Jamie was noticeably nervous; he kept rubbing his palms against his pants and constantly checking his phone for the time. They'd left early and had more than enough time, but this was such a huge appointment for him that he didn't want to be even a moment late.

"It's gonna be fine," Nate reassured him, but Jamie just smiled at him nervously and said nothing.

As soon as they arrived at the facility, Jamie headed to the reception desk to get the paperwork sorted out. Raziel sat down on one of the couches, and Nate hesitated, thinking maybe he should sit in his own chair. But he craved being close to Raziel, so he sat down next to him. As their knees touched, a shiver went through his body. It was silly, really. They slept next to each other every single night. But this felt different for some reason.

To distract himself, Nate focused on Jamie, who was walking toward them. He sat down in one of the surprisingly comfortable chairs next to them, his leg bobbing up and down, his eyes darting around the room. Nate gently put one hand on Jamie's knee, hoping to calm him.

"It'll be fine," he said encouragingly. "You have all your documents. You'll finally get your T and then you'll get a deeper voice and grow a beard. It'll all work out."

Jamie took a deep breath, held it for a moment, and then exhaled. "I know, it's just so...unreal. I never thought I'd actually get this far."

Nate squeezed his hand. "I know this sort of thing can be nerve-wracking, but it'll be worth it."

When Jamie's name was called, he almost jumped up and went with the nurse, leaving Nate and Raz out in the waiting room. While Jamie was in the room, Nate scrolled through social media, but it got kind of boring pretty fast. Instead, he watched Raziel, who's face was buried in his own phone. Somehow, he still managed to looked incredibly handsome, even just staring at the little screen in front of him. Nate was impressed by how fast he'd adjusted to being human and doing silly human things, like posting pretty selfies on his stories, which Nate always stared at a little too long.

"Your piercing's healed really well," he realized while he was still staring.

Raziel had gotten one some time ago, a bridge piercing right between his eyes, and it fit him incredibly well, like it belonged there, accentuating his green eyes.

Raz looked up and brushed his hair aside to have a clear view—and it gave Nate a better look onto the angel's face, the soft looking lips he sometimes dreamed about.

"It did," Raz said. "I was told it takes longer to fully heal, even if it looks healed already, so I gotta take good care of it still. I like it, too."

Raziel smiled at him, and Nate's heartbeat sped up. That smile was beautiful. *Everything* about Raziel was beautiful. Slowly, Nate realized he might have already fallen in love with the angel. He'd never imagined having such an attractive man around all the time—not just attractive but also such a gentle soul. Living so close together had made it harder for Nate not to fall for him, and if he didn't want to drown in those dark green eyes, framed by light hair, he would have to say something—*anything*—to break his own stare.

"Do you miss Heaven at all?" he asked, whispering so the other two people in the waiting room wouldn't hear.

Raz leaned back and crossed his legs as he stared at the opposite wall, contemplating. It was an intimate question; Nate knew as much, and he almost regretted asking, but he was curious. Would Raziel want to go back if he got the chance? Would he leave Nate without a second thought?

"Not really," Raziel said. "Earth is much more intense in a lot of ways, and I like being here." After a few quiet moments, he added, "I was thrown out for things I didn't do, exiled by my own family. I don't want to go back to that. I prefer being here, with you and Jamie. It might not be the most interesting life, but it's *my* life, and I get to make decisions on my own now." Raziel tilted his head to Nate, a crooked smile on his full lips. "Truth be told, my memories of Heaven have started to blur anyway."

Nate hadn't expected that answer, and he stared at Raz, stunned by his honest words. But he also understood. There was no way he'd want to go back to a family that judged him unfairly and tossed him out, scarring him mentally and physically. With a bitter chuckle, he realized he'd lived through exactly the same thing, just on a smaller scale. Both their scars proved how fucked up their families were.

"I know it's not the best life I can offer," Nate said, "and I'm pretty fucked up myself, but I'm still glad you feel that way."

A sheepish smile covered Nate's face. Maybe it was egoistical to revel in the thought of Raziel enjoying his time here because of him, but for once he wanted to be egoistical, wanted to feel loved and desired. He was just human—and humans needed love.

"I don't mind that you're fucked up," the angel said. "I like being around you...a lot."

Now Raziel smiled at him, a smirk that made his heart beat faster and his cheeks heat up. The soft hand unexpectedly settling above his knee didn't really make it any better, and warmth spread from Nate's stomach throughout his whole body.

Nate was spared from having to say anything because Jamie was rushing over to them, grinning from one ear to the other. "I got my first shot!" Jamie announced proudly.

Immediately, Nate got up to hug his best friend tight—although he already missed Raziel's warm hand on his leg.

For once, life seemed to be working out. Maybe it wasn't so bad after all.

CHAPTER ELEVEN
Can I Keep You

After Jamie's appointment, they went to get some food, and for once, Nate didn't protest when Jamie ordered a burger for each of them. Nate even ate all of it, even the fries, and despite feeling really stuffed now, he wasn't sick. Instead, he was looking forward to going to a club. How long had it been since he'd been in one? With the pandemic, tonight was probably the first time in years.

Once it was dark outside and their favorite club was open, they headed there and got their first round of drinks. It was still rather empty inside, but people crowded the club fast, dancing to the loud music, most of them clad in black or other dark colors. They fit in perfectly—Jamie wore his metal chain collar, with the same kind of black clothes and boots Nate was wearing, and Raziel had chosen Nate's favorite black ripped jeans and another tight, dark red shirt. Nate glanced at him and noticed that Raz had opened some more of his shirt buttons, so he got a glance at his smooth chest. Fuck, the angel looked so good.

As far as Nate knew, Raziel hadn't had any alcohol yet, and he wondered if the angel wanted to try some today. "How about you? Whiskey-coke, too?" Nate asked as he stood at the bar and waited for his own drink.

"Let me try yours first," Raz suggested, distracting Nate a bit from how gorgeous he was as he took the cup from his hands to try a sip. Then he nodded. "I'll just keep that," the angel teased.

He was standing behind Nate, close enough that they were almost touching. Nate could feel his body heat, and he wondered if the heat on his face came from the sticky air in the room or from being so close to Raz

Luckily, the bartender distracted him as she handed him two cups filled to the brim—one for Jamie and one for himself.

"To you, Jamie," he said, raising his glass after paying for the drinks, "and to a new stage of your life. Prost!"

With a grin, he took a big sip from his own drink, the sweetness of coke and bitterness of the alcohol mixing on his tongue. Yes, this was good. Nate had needed this evening out more than he realized. The cool drink and alcohol, the music and bass vibrating through his body, and the lights illuminating everything in blue and red hues—it all relaxed him, and for once, no thoughts occupied his mind.

For a while, Nate just watched people dance. Jamie had joined them, enjoying the evening, moving with the music. Most times, Nate didn't like dancing; he was too insecure for it, of what people might think of him, He worried that they'd judge him. Only when he was really drunk and wasn't thinking anymore would he join the dance floor. Until then, Nate preferred to just enjoy the vibe.

It was much more interesting to watch Raziel dance, the angel's half-empty drink in one hand, eyes closed, body moving to the music. It looked like the most natural thing in the world to Nate, and he couldn't stop staring. Right here, in a club, Raziel had an even more angelic appearance than Nate had ever seen before.

Blue and red hues danced across his face, his red shirt almost black in the dim light, and Nate was sure he must be drooling already.

As Raziel opened his eyes and looked directly at him, Nate blushed violently. Good thing the light in here was so dim; hopefully Raz wouldn't see his blush. He turned around sharply and downed his cup before he headed to the bathroom to pee and wash his face with cold water. Most times it helped him calm down a little, get his emotions under control. When his cheeks stopped burning as much, Nate left the bathroom and was startled by the voice greeting him.

"I got you a new drink." Raz was leaning against the wall next to the door and smiling at him, a filled cup in his hand.

Judging from the look of it, it was probably a beer, but any drink was a welcome relief right now.

"Uhm, thanks." A bit awkwardly, Nate smiled at the angel and took the cup. Greedily, he took a big gulp and coughed immediately.

Shit, now this was even more embarrassing. It took him a moment to gather himself, and he was glad Raziel had grabbed the cup until his cough subsided. Looking up again, he realized the cup was almost halfway empty, and Raziel's cheeky grin was reason enough to believe he'd drunk some of the beer, too, before offering it back to Nate, who drank the rest.

"Come, I want to dance with you," Raz urged him and took his hand.

Before Nate could protest, they were already on the dance floor, where Raz took his second hand as well and moved with him. Slowly, he relaxed, trusting Raz to guide him if he was unsure, and the more they danced, the more he leaned into this feeling of freedom, the vibrations of the music, and Raziel's body heat pressed against him.

The angel's hands were on his hips, and Nate had to admit, it felt so good. He didn't think anymore, just enjoyed every moment of being so close to Raz, of feeling him like this. How did an angel know how to dance so well? Just for a moment, he wondered, before he was gently turned around and now faced said angel.

The light made the golden speckles in Raziel's eyes sparkle even more, almost like stars in the night sky, mesmerizing him. Nate couldn't, didn't want to, think, just wanted to be in the moment. Raziel's palm on his cheek radiated warmth, and he brushed some strands of blue hair aside. Nate could only stare, frozen in place, anticipation prickling in his fingers, as his gaze wandered down to Raziel's lips. There was a smirk, and Raz leaned closer, his full lips pressing against Nate's.

Even if Nate wanted to think, no thought was left. Instead, he leaned into the kiss, his arms around Raziel's neck to keep him from ever going away again. This was all he needed, all he wanted: to be loved by someone good, someone who really cared about him.

Again and again, Raziel kissed him, until every doubt and worry was gone. They just stood there, completely focused on each other—at least until a girl bumped into them, parting them for a moment as Nate struggled to keep his balance.

"Sorry!" She grinned and just kept dancing.

Worry and frustration immediately flashed up in Nate. What if this had been a one-time thing? What if Raz regretted kissing him? Once separated, would it be the only time? Although the moment had been so beautiful, Nate started doubting everything, couldn't stop his mind from wandering off. Even Raziel's chuckle and the squeeze of his hand didn't help much.

"Let's get another drink and go outside," Raz whispered into his ear and gently pulled him to the bar, where he ordered two more beers. One hand was still holding Nate's, and it reassured him a bit.

He still wondered if Raziel actually wanted this, or if he was just drunk. Did it really matter? In this moment, Nate didn't care. He would just lean into it, whatever this was, and enjoy the moment.

With beer in hand, the other one still occupied by Raz, he followed the angel to a small patio. He wondered how Raz knew about this place, but did it matter? Not really. What mattered was Raziel, who pulled him to a wooden sunbed covered by a plush pillow, with a small table next to it.

After a glance around, Nate knew no one else was outside. Even better. He liked being alone with Raz, especially after what had happened on the dance floor. Raziel sat down and placed his glass on the table, then he smiled and stretched out his hand to Nate, inviting him to come closer. Nate understood that, and he hurried to accept the invitation.

Nate sat on the angel's lap. A warm hand found its place on his hip, and the other wandered higher, to his neck, to gently pull him down into another kiss. Even though Nate wanted to enjoy the kiss, he leaned back a little, just enough to look at Raz. Before this could continue, he wanted to be sure of one thing.

"Are you drunk?" Nate asked. Although Nate himself was a little tipsy, he wasn't drunk—not after eating so much and his body being used to alcohol—but that didn't mean Raz wasn't.

"I don't think so," Raz said, looking up to him. "I told you. I like you."

How couldn't he believe Raz? With such a genuine and charming smile, the angel could probably tell him a thousand lies, and he would willingly believe them.

"Can you promise this isn't just a one-time thing for tonight?" Nate pressed on, almost desperate. He didn't want to get used again.

"I promise," Raz said. "I'll want to kiss you tomorrow, too."

It was all Nate needed, the reassurance he craved. Of course, Raz could be lying, could promise him the stars from the sky and not deliver the next day. The angel might even use his tipsy state to his advantage. But there had been better moments to do so, Nate realized, and Raz had never done it then.

Nate trusted Raz deeply, and he knew he'd never get abused by him. It was the reason he leaned down again to kiss Raziel, more desperately and with more longing than before. He had wished for this the last days—weeks. To feel so loved and wanted.

No matter how Raz touched him, the angel always kept his hands above his clothes, being modest, remembering they weren't all alone. It didn't stop Nate's body from reacting, but he didn't really care.

Nate wasn't sure how long they kissed, but his lips prickled pleasantly. He had laid down on Raziel, his head resting on Raziel's chest, where the angel's heartbeat mixed with the music and bass he could still hear from inside the club. Raziel's fingers were in his hair, gently stroking it, and Nate was so deeply relaxed, he could fall asleep in this position at any moment.

"We should head home. It's getting cold, and we're both tired," Raziel said.

Although he was right, Nate wasn't really willing to let go and get up yet. He whined when the angel tried to sit up.

"It's alright, Nate. I won't let go or leave. I promise." Raz smiled at him. "When we're home, I'll kiss you more."

The words were spoken so softly, Nate just had to believe them. Raziel's loving smile as he looked up only confirmed his trust. After another kiss, Nate slowly got up and grabbed their empty cups. As promised, the angel's fingers entwined themselves with his own as soon as Raziel was up.

A smile covered Nate's face while they headed inside. They wanted to wait for Jamie, since they didn't want to leave him here without at least telling him they were leaving. Once Jamie spotted them, he headed to them and stared at their hands, a broad grin on his face.

"A good day for all of us, huh?" Jamie said.

Nate could only agree—a good day indeed.

Chapter Twelve

First Times

OCTOBER 1ST, 2023

Even though Raziel was still holding Nate's hand and never let go on their way home on the bus, what had happened felt unreal to Nate. They'd actually kissed. Raziel really liked him this way. How did he deserve such an amazing person liking him?

Raziel didn't let him think about it too much, kissing him again and again, small pecks on his cheek, his forehead, his lips, everywhere he could reach, and held him close to make sure he wasn't freezing too much. It had gotten quite cold, and as the warming effect of the alcohol dwindled, Nate started shivering slightly.

He was glad when they were home in their little apartment, the door closing behind them. Good thing the warmth of the sunlight was still trapped inside the room, making it cozy enough. Soon, he'd have to turn up the heater.

A bit sluggish, Nate got rid of his jacket and boots, and as soon as he had, Raziel's lips were on his own again, and he was gently pushed onto the bed.

Almost desperately, Nate held onto the angel's shirt, keeping him close, even when he felt the mattress against his back and Raziel's weight on him. It was so much better than it had ever been with Daniel. He knew Raz would never hurt him, would stop if he asked him to, but did he want him to stop?

His mind was still clouded, his judgment gone to another place. Only pure emotions and raw desperation to finally be loved and cared for were left inside him. He didn't care if he would regret any of this tomorrow. Right now, it was good and right.

Slowly, his hands found their way to Raziel's shirt, unbuttoning it, baring more of the angel's skin. Not that he saw much with the way Raz was smothering him with kisses, trapping him with those soft, gentle lips.

As Raziel's hand found its way underneath his own shirt, Nate tensed up.

"Don't. Not the shirt," he mumbled against Raz's lips, begging him not to take it off. No matter how much he trusted Raziel, he didn't want him to see the scars, didn't want him to be disgusted.

Green eyes met his, worried and yet so caring. It felt like Raziel was looking right into his soul, through all the layers and walls Nate had built over years, but it wasn't uncomfortable. It was reassuring to know Raz cared for him so much, made sure he was comfortable, and saw him for who he really was.

"It's alright, I won't," the angel whispered and leaned down again to kiss his neck instead.

With a pleased whine, Nate stretched his neck, offering it up to Raz. It was an incredibly vulnerable thing, especially after what had happened with Daniel, but there was so much trust between them that he didn't hesitate.

His hands blindly searched for the button for Raziel's pants. Heat surged through him when Raz licked his neck, right underneath his ear. His neck was so sensitive, and somehow Raz knew exactly how to touch and kiss him to make him feel good. As Raz kissed and licked his neck, Nate melted from the attention. Nothing about this felt wrong or brought up bad memories; the only thing on Nate's mind was the angel.

When Raziel caught his lips in a longing kiss again, Nate managed to pull on his shirt in a desperate try to get rid of it. Raziel broke the kiss and smirked at him, then got up from the bed. Curiously, Nate watched as he took off his shirt and pants—and underwear. He hadn't seen Raz completely naked since finding him, and seeing him now in all his glory was mesmerizing. Even if he tried to, he couldn't pry his gaze from Raz's middle, ready for anything to come, and his own pants were tight already as well. Everything about Raz was beautiful, and Nate still couldn't believe this wonderful man was interested in someone as boring and broken as *him*.

But there was nothing in Raziel's actions or expression to suggest that he was only playing him, and Nate trusted him not to. The angel smiled and leaned down to draw him into another kiss as he undid Nate's pants and pulled them down, taking his underwear with them.

Just a moment later, the angel found his way between Nate's willingly spread legs and pressed against him. The intimacy of the contact and the knowledge of how much Raz wanted him coaxed a moan from Nate's lips. It was silenced immediately by another kiss, more longing and passionate than the ones before.

They both were desperate for this.

Nate wouldn't stop it from happening.

Instead, he wrapped his legs around Raziel's hip, keeping him as close as possible. His hands explored the soft skin up from Raz's shoulders, over the scars on his back, and down to his ass.

It all was a blur—Raz grabbing the lube from the nightstand, his teasing fingers everywhere they could reach, the condom he conjured up from somewhere—until they were finally one, moving together. Sex had never felt so good for Nate, so painless and liberating. Raz knew exactly what he was doing, was gentle and yet firm in his thrusts, kissed his lips, his neck, even his wrists, while he held his hands tightly. It gave Nate the reassurance he wasn't being used but actually cared for, actually *loved*, and the knowledge aroused him even more.

It didn't take long for Nate to moan the angel's name in passion, all his pleasure releasing at once. Two, three breaths later, he could hear Raziel moan as well, such a beautiful noise. From that moment on, Nate knew he would never get enough of this, of Raziel.

Neither would he ever get enough of the kisses Raziel gave him while he clung to the angel, arms wrapped around him tightly. Nothing else mattered, just the two of them were important.

Even when they fell asleep, the angel hugging him from behind, arms wrapped around his chest, Nate was completely relaxed, more than he had been in a *long* time. He was loved.

A MOVEMENT WOKE UP Nate the next morning. A complaining whine followed, and he held onto whatever was moving under his head. Only slowly, he realized it was an arm. A moment later, he heard a chuckle, and the movement stilled, then he was pressed against a warm body and held tightly.

"Sorry, didn't want to wake you," Raziel whispered and kissed his shoulder through his t-shirt.

It took Nate a moment to remember what had happened, and as he did, his cheeks got warm. Especially once he realized they were still naked underneath the blanket. They really had slept with each other.

And now he didn't know what to say. Nate was overwhelmed by the situation, had no experience with this; there had only been hook-ups or Daniel, and Daniel had never been as loving with him as Raz was.

"Did you sleep well?" the angel asked, and Nate could only nod.

For once, his body didn't hurt after a night of sex. Instead, he was relaxed. He shuffled around a little and turned, still in Raz's hug, so he could look at the angel. The light hair was completely messy, and a soft smile was on Raziel's lips—soft lips, as Nate knew by now. Carefully, he pushed back some strands to see Raz's face even better. Even in the morning, after such a long night, he was beautiful.

Nate still didn't know how he deserved such a handsome and caring man, and he was afraid to fuck it up. Sooner or later, he'd scare off Raziel, once the angel realized how beyond repair he actually was. But shouldn't he still enjoy the time they had until then? Would it matter if his heart got broken once more? It was already cracked; what would one more tear do?

If he was lucky, Raz would mend some damage, handle his heart with care—if anyone could, it was Raz.

"Before you ask," Raziel said, "I don't regret anything. I promised, I'll want to kiss you today, too. And I do—*more* than just kiss."

Raz's smirk distracted Nate from his thoughts and made him blush but also chuckle softly. He was just glad Raziel wasn't someone who only used an opportunity and left right afterward, someone who made empty promises. Nate knew the worries came from his own mind, and it wasn't fair to doubt Raz, especially since he hadn't given Nate any reason to. But convincing himself that he was safe was hard.

Nate had been staring into space, but finally, he said, "Alright, but no kisses before brushing teeth, not after how much we partied last night."

Raz didn't seem to notice anything was off. There was a big grin on the angel's face, and he leaned closer and kissed Nate's neck before looking at him. "Then we better get up! I'll go shower first."

Raziel got up and stretched, still smiling. He obviously didn't give a damn that Nate could see him fully naked, and Nate couldn't stop his eyes from wandering once more from the firm ass up to his shoulders, where he spotted the scars he'd felt underneath his fingers yesterday. Maybe he should show Raziel his own ones as well—but not yet. He wasn't ready for it, no matter how much he trusted Raz.

He was still too worried that he'd scare Raz off. Nate didn't want to be alone again, trapped in a loveless relationship, only used and abused. It could be different with Raziel. The thought was intriguing, interesting and yet scary. How did a healthy relationship work? Nate didn't know, not from experience, and it scared him even more. There was no point in worrying about all that now; they'd only slept together once. But Nate was a pro at distracting himself until the point that all his thoughts came crashing down at once.

With the calming rush of the shower in background, he rubbed his eyes and finally sat up. When he'd found his underwear and put it on, he took a look at his phone, remembering they would have to work later. With an annoyed groan he checked the clock. Good, they still had two hours left.

But first he had some messages from Jamie, which made him smile a bit again.

> got home safe?

> what's up with you and raz?

> i need to know all the juicy details!

Of course, Jamie was dying to know what happened. He hadn't expected anything different from his terminally curious best friend. Still, with a mischievous smile, Nate wondered if he should answer immediately or let Jamie wait some more. Finally, he decided to text a short reply.

> you're nosy
> gonna tell you later

This wasn't the sort of thing he wanted to talk about over text. But he *would* tell him. He needed Jamie's help to sort through his thoughts and worries. All of this was a little much for him. Especially once Raziel left the bathroom, a towel wrapped around his waist and another around his hair.

"Shower's free. I'll make some breakfast."

Nate nodded and grabbed fresh underwear and a shirt from his wardrobe before he headed to the bathroom. Before he reached the door, he was gently stopped by a hand around his wrist, and just a moment later, Raziel's lips were on his own, greeting him with a soft kiss.

"Now you can go," Raziel said with a smile and let go of his arm. The angel turned to the wardrobe, while Nate blushed and hurried into the bathroom, looking forward to a long shower.

Being treated so lovingly and with such care was new for him. Sure, he'd had a relationship before Daniel, but that was in his teens. Honestly, it couldn't even be called relationship; he'd just made out a bit with his crush, nothing more. Raziel was different. He was more like a dream come true, and Nate wondered what it would be that turned this dream into a nightmare. He'd learned long ago that nothing good lasted forever.

Would it be his own mind fucking him over? Daniel showing up at the worst moment? Or would it be Raziel's still somewhat mysterious past? Maybe something completely different? There were too many options, and Nate didn't want to dwell on them, or he'd spiral. But they were still there, still poking at his mind, threatening to tarnish the beautiful night he and Raz had spent together and the lovely morning they'd just shared.

After his shower, he got dressed and sat down on the sofa with Raziel, who handed him a bowl of cereal. It wasn't a fancy breakfast, but the angel had given it his best and had also made some tea for him. These small gestures showed him how much Raz cared, that he actually remembered what Nate liked.

"Do angels have sex?" Nate wondered to himself. When Raz laughed, he realized he'd actually asked his question out loud.

"Are you asking me if I was a virgin before last night?" Raziel teased him a little, and although it was embarrassing, Nate nodded, his eyes fixed on his bowl of cereal. "That's a secret I'll keep to myself. Does it matter?"

Did it? Not really. Either Raziel had some experience, or he just knew very well what to do. It wasn't really important. And yet, Nate couldn't help but wonder what other secrets Raz was keeping from him. He should trust Raz fully, but a nagging voice in his head wondered if Raz trusted *him* fully.

Only time would tell.

Chapter Thirteen

 Guardian

Life was actually worth living for once. Being around Raziel, dating him, was such a good feeling. The last days, even weeks, Nate hadn't drunk much or hurt himself, and it was such a big improvement for him. He even ate regularly, whenever Raziel did, and had gained a little weight. He'd even started calling his grandma again, which he hadn't thought to do in weeks. Or, really, he'd been avoiding doing it, which he felt guilty about.

Nate just hadn't had enough energy for all this before. The constant fear and worry of when Daniel might text and demand a painful "date" had exhausted him—numbed him. Nate only slowly learned to relax and enjoy his life with Raziel by his side.

"You got the whole shift today, right?" Raziel wondered while he looked through Nate's bookshelf, interested in the little trinkets and books. They had spent the morning in bed, just cuddling—Nate drawing and Raz finishing up his current read.

"Yeah, and I guess we'll have more customers today. It's raining."

Generally, fall and winter were the busiest time, and Nate wouldn't work alone today.

"Which one should I read next?" Raz wondered, gesturing to the books.

Nate came closer. It was amazing to see Raziel's fascination with modern pop culture, and they had already watched some movies together. Raz also liked reading and had already devoured some of the books on his shelf.

"Try this one. It's about a vampire and a warlock and some weird time travel. Jamie gave it to me because he got himself a second copy signed by the author." And, as so often happened, gifted Nate the duplicate edition. He had read a few interesting books because of this.

"Sounds intriguing." The angel took the book from the shelf and stored it in a pouch Jamie had also gifted Nate, so books wouldn't get damaged when stuffing them into a backpack.

"Do vampires and warlocks and werewolves actually exist?" Nate asked. If angels existed, maybe those creatures did as well? Who would know better than an actual angel?

Raz just shrugged and put the pouch in his messenger bag. The angel had really embraced the whole alternative look and mostly clad himself in black and dark colors, including not giving a damn about other people's opinions on his black nail polish or piercings. "Not that I'm aware of, but I'm not all-knowing. There are things out there I don't know about. Maybe other creatures exist, maybe not. Angels and demons do for sure."

This was the first Nate had heard about demons. It made sense, of course, for them to exist next to angels. He still had no idea how to imagine Heaven and Hell, but every time he'd asked Raziel, the angel had just smiled and redirected the conversation, not answering any of his questions.

Nate had learned not to pry, though he burned with curiosity. Maybe someday Raz would feel comfortable telling Nate everything.

He hoped.

WORK REALLY WAS CRAZY today, with so many customers coming in that he barely had time to refill the beverage fridge for the next round of movies.

"I'll get us some food," Raz said. "What do you want?"

Raz was leaning on the counter, waiting for an answer. He'd stopped in to see Nate. His hair was wet, as were his clothes, because it'd been raining all day. Nate tried to remember if he owned an umbrella, then realized Raz was looking at him expectantly.

"Whatever you want. Thanks, love." He leaned into Raz and got a gentle kiss that made him smile before the angel turned to the door. "Oh, and can you get me an energy drink?" Nate remembered.

Raziel turned around halfway, before he nodded and waved his hand, leaving the cinema with a smile.

"Y'know I'm a bit jealous," Percy said as he refilled the popcorn. He was a coworker who Nate had known for several years now. "You've got such a hot and caring boyfriend. Where did you find him anyway?"

"By accident," Nate admitted. "We met at the abandoned factory outside the city, and at first, I thought he was a junkie." He chuckled at how silly he'd been. "Turns out, he's just a weirdo. A very lovely one."

One he had really fallen for. Raziel had changed his life for the better, and despite how weird it all was, the angel had adjusted fine to living a human life, no matter how boring it often was.

"Guess I gotta hang out there more. But considering my bad luck, I'll just find actual junkies." Percy sighed deeply before he grinned. "He wouldn't have some pretty friends? Or brothers?"

Actually, that was a good question. Were angels more like friends to each other? Or family? Kundaliel had called Raziel "brother." Another question about Heaven he'd love to ask Raziel, but he wasn't sure if he'd get an answer.

"Don't think so, sorry."

He smiled at Percy who just shrugged. Nate was grateful for the customers pouring into the foyer again, demanding attention. He'd take any distraction from this conversation that he could get.

TIDYING UP AFTER THE last movie took a long time today, and Nate was glad Raziel came back to help them, carrying around crates of bottles even though he was off today so they could head home faster. He was exhausted and glad when they were at their bus stop.

"Can we watch a movie tonight? Something really dumb or trashy?" Nate asked. He wanted to just cuddle with Raziel for the rest of the evening with something mindless on in the background.

Raziel chuckled and put an arm around his shoulder, pulling him close and kissing his temple. "Sure, trashy is good. I gotta get to know all the terrible movies."

When they turned toward the entrance of their home, Nate stopped. Someone was lurking at the door. *Shit.* Not *him.* Not *now.* Since Jamie had blocked Daniel's number, Nate hadn't seen him for quite some time. He'd hoped Daniel would just give up, but here he stood, waiting for him. And Nate just wanted to run far away.

"There you are, bitch!" Daniel seethed. "Who's that fucker? That the one you cheated on me with? I gotta show you who's a real man and where you belong!"

This couldn't be happening now, not when his life was finally good. Nate was numb, unable to move or talk. Just seeing Daniel brought painful memories back, and his hands started trembling. He didn't want to get hurt again, didn't want Daniel to touch him.

His panic mixed with worry about Raziel. His ex wasn't afraid to use violence, and Nate didn't want to drag Raziel into all this. It was *his* problem, not Raz's.

"You should go," Nate whispered, his eyes fixed on Daniel, who approached them.

But the angel made no move to leave. On the contrary, he pulled Nate behind himself. Nate tore his gaze from Daniel to see Raz's angry face, the angel's eyes fixed on the approaching man.

"Better leave Nathaniel alone, or I'll make you."

Despite the words, Raziel's voice was calm, though it had a threatening undertone, which would only make Daniel more furious. For a moment, Nate wondered why Raz was protecting him, why he didn't look out for himself instead. Nate had endured this shit with Daniel for long enough to know how to dissociate, but

Raziel didn't, and Nate wanted to keep him safe from his messed up past.

Daniel charged, throwing a punch at Raz. Without thinking about it, Nate tried to jump between them to shield Raziel. It was his problem, his fault, and Raziel shouldn't pay the price for it. It didn't matter that Nate had no experience with fights. If he was just a punching bag for Daniel, it was alright too—as long as Raz didn't get hurt.

A strong punch hit his side, and Nate doubled up with a choked whine. Another hand pushed him aside, gentle yet firm. He stumbled a few steps away and watched what was going on. Utter helplessness rushed through him. He wasn't strong enough to help Raz, nor could he even react. His body was numb, his limbs not following his commands.

For a moment, it looked like Daniel had the upper-hand, and Nate was afraid what he'd do to Raz. Why did it have to come to this? Why couldn't Daniel just leave him alone? And why did Raz have to get pulled into this whole shit show?

Relief rushed through him when Raz threw some well-placed punches, and his ex ended up reeling on the ground, cursing and glaring at Raz. The angel got down on one knee and grabbed Daniel's neck firmly, to press him down into the ground.

"If you ever come close to Nate again, I won't be so lenient," Raz warned. "I'll send you straight to Hell."

Just for a moment, Nate thought the golden speckles in Raz's eyes grew bigger, shining down bright on his now huffing and groaning ex. But maybe it was just the light. It didn't matter. What was important was that Raziel was safe.

When Raz got up again, he pushed back his hair and grabbed his bag before leading Nate to the door. One last glance at Daniel revealed he'd already sat up and was staring at them with hatred. Hopefully this would be the last time they saw him.

Once they were safely inside with the door locked behind them, Nate slowly relaxed. His body was shaking, and his stomach hurt. Nausea mixed with a pulsing headache, and only now he realized Raz was bleeding, his lip split open.

"You're bleeding. Sit down."

It was only a whisper, and Nate didn't look at Raz when he hurried into the kitchen to wet some paper towels. Back in the living room, Raz had sat down on the couch, so Nate could carefully press the damp towels against his lip, trying to stem the bleeding.

He wasn't sure what to say. Raziel had protected him, stood up to Daniel. He had fought to keep him safe because Nate couldn't do it himself. If Daniel had gotten to him alone, this would have ended very differently. Nate would've preferred that. He wouldn't have endangered Raz, and it wouldn't have been the first time Daniel hurt him.

"I'm sorry. I'm so sorry," Nate whispered, tears welling up.

The shivering got stronger, and it was hard to hold the paper towel. Raziel took the towel from his fingers and wrapped an arm around his shoulder to pull him close.

"There's nothing to apologize for," Raz assured him. "It's not your fault this guy's a dick. As long as I can protect you, I will. Always."

A soft kiss was placed on his temple despite Raz's surely hurting lip. Nate leaned his head against the angel's chest, and hearing his heartbeat soothed Nate, reminded him to take deep, slow breaths. Unfortunately, it did nothing to calm his mind, self-blame circling with worry and anger over his own uselessness. But Nate was okay. He was alive. They both were. And that was what mattered. Swallowing hard and pushing away his self-deprecating thoughts, he said, "Thank you for protecting me."

CHAPTER FOURTEEN

My Demons

OCTOBER 16TH, 2023

That night he was haunted by nightmares, and Nate barely slept. He spent half the night awake, staring at the ceiling, hoping to escape the hellhole his mind was becoming once again. Despite Raziel being right beside him, he was feeling like shit, and thoughts were circling in his brain. If not for him, Raziel wouldn't have been hurt. He should have dealt with his problems on his own and not dragged someone else into this mess as well.

Guilt-ridden, his gaze wandered to the angel next to him, illuminated by the moonlight shining into their apartment. Carefully, his fingertips traced Raz's cheek and jaw until they came to a rest on his chest. Sleep wouldn't come to him again tonight, so he better use the time to enjoy being so close to Raziel. One could never know how much time together they had.

THE NEXT MORNING, RAZ was already dressed for work.

"Sure you don't want to come with me?" Raziel asked. Nate had a free day today and had decided to stay at home while Raz was working. He wasn't sure if it was the best idea, but he would try to sleep some more. He was just so damn exhausted. Every limb was numb, and he could barely keep his eyes open.

"Yeah, I'll sleep a little or watch a movie. I'll be fine."

He smiled at the angel tiredly and leaned into the kiss he was given. He would find some kind of distraction to stop his looping thoughts. He had to before it drove him crazy.

"If you need anything, call me or Jamie, alright?" Raz said. "Doesn't matter when or why."

Nate just nodded and watched Raziel leave, the angel throwing one last worried gaze over his shoulder. Nate still wondered if he'd imagined the golden glimmer last night or if it had been real. Not that it really mattered. He was just tired and didn't give a damn about anything at the moment.

Right now, he would just try to sleep a little and headed to the bed, where he cuddled himself up into the blanket that smelled so welcoming, like Raz. Dozing off a little, he relaxed.

Until the nightmares and memories came back.

Daniel beating Raziel right in front of him, again and again until the angel lay motionless on the ground, bleeding and barely breathing, before Daniel's dark brown eyes fixated on him.

Nate was on his bed, pain emanating from his shoulders and back, the smell of cold smoke and burning flesh filling his nose, his lungs, until he thought he couldn't breathe anymore. It was choking him, like Daniel's hand around his throat had.

With a jolt, Nate woke up and looked around, but Daniel was nowhere to be seen. No cigarettes or smoke either. *Just a nightmare.* And still, it had been real. It all had happened, the cigarettes, the burns, the choking—even Raziel bleeding because of him.

An overwhelming and crushing wave of guilt and helplessness rushed over him, leaving him gasping for air, a heavy weight pressing against his chest and clouding his mind.

His fault. It was all his fault for being so weak. He didn't deserve Raziel or his love. He should've known; his father had taught him that for so many years. He wasn't worthy of love, just pain and being used as an ashtray. A worthless slut.

You'll never forget me.

Daniel's voice was too clear in his mind, haunting him. He was right—Nate would *never* forget him. Daniel had made sure of that. But Nate wanted to forget, wanted his mind to be quiet, wanted to stop this downward spiral of misery that threatened to drown him.

Without giving it another thought, Nate got up and scuffled into the kitchen, where he grabbed his bottle of Jägermeister. On his way back to the bed, he took a big sip. The dark liquid ran down his throat, the comforting warmth burning slightly.

He hadn't felt so bad for weeks, not since Daniel's last visit, but seeing him had destroyed all of the progress he'd made toward healing and thrown him right back into the never-ending abyss.

His mental demons didn't give him a break, reminded him again and again of how worthless he was, how he was unable to find a good job or be cared for by his family. They didn't give a fuck about him. Surely, his grandma only kept in contact with him for obligatory reasons, not because she actually cared. Who could care about a fuck-up like him?

Every sip of alcohol made his mind wonkier, but the numbness was worse. His limbs didn't look like his anymore. They moved, but was it really Nate who controlled them? Did it even matter? He was only a puppet for others to play with.

Why couldn't it all just stop? All the pain and worry and guilt? He couldn't even cry. He just wanted it all to stop, wanted his head, the voices inside, to stop screaming at him.

Slowly, with numb fingers, he searched through his nightstand and found the small hidden box in the back corner. Trembling, he opened it and grabbed the glass shard from it. No doubts crossed his mind, only relief that he had a way out of this spiral and numbness.

He pressed the sharp edge against his left forearm, where it left a small trail of blood. He barely felt the pain. Another cut followed. The blade found its way onto his arm again and again until one cut made him pant lowly, sweet pain emanating from the fresh wound. It was a dull one, not nearly as vivid as the red blood pouring down his pale skin.

Two last sips from his bottle emptied it, and he fell back on the bed. With unfocused eyes, he stared at the ceiling and didn't care if he was still bleeding or not. He hoped he was. The slight burning around the cut dulled the pain in his heart, his soul.

Finally, he could sleep. Finally, he could find peace.

"Nate! NATE! Come on, wake up! Please!"

He was harshly awoken from his slumber to find Raziel leaning over him, panic on his face.

"Shit, Nate, you scared me!"

He felt the angel's hand around his arm, firmly pressing a towel against the skin. He barely remembered what'd happened. Why was Raziel so distraught? Confused, he looked up at him, searching for an answer.

"I thought you were gone," Raz whispered and pulled him closer with his free hand, holding him against his chest.

Slowly, Nate's gaze wandered to his arm, and now he could see the white towel was stained with red spots. Once he remembered, the pain also came back, piece by piece, no longer fully dulled by the alcohol.

"I...didn't want to..."

His voice broke, and he halted. Had he? Wanted to go? He wasn't so sure. He hadn't cared at all, just wanted the worries and doubts to stop. Still, he was glad he wasn't gone and could feel Raz holding him now. Day by day, he was becoming his own worst enemy, and his inner demons were taking over. Even with a literal angel by his side, he couldn't stop them from tearing him apart from the inside.

"Shh, it's okay. I've got you," Raz said soothingly. "I'm letting go for a moment to get a wet towel and bandage, alright? But I'll be back in half a minute. Here, hold this for me, would you?"

Nate nodded slowly as his head was placed onto a pillow, his hand directed to the towel around his left forearm. Instinctively, he pressed the fabric against his skin, though not as tight as Raziel had. He was too exhausted for that.

Awake again, his mind started throwing doubts at him again. Why did Raz care for him so much? Did he only want a willing toy as well? No, Raziel wasn't like that. Or was he? Nate wasn't sure about anything anymore. His thoughts were circling, a hellish carousel of self-hatred, painful memories, and doubts about the future. It'd be much easier for Raziel if he wasn't here anymore. Raz would find someone else. He was a great guy who could make connections easily. He should've just run and let Nate slip away.

But instead of running, the angel was hurrying through the apartment and was back at his side soon. He sat down and gently took away the towel to wipe off all the blood. Nate silently watched his actions, but he didn't feel much of Raziel's touch, his limbs still numb. One cut was still bleeding lightly, fresh drops of deep red blood running over his skin and staining the towel even more.

Nate observed Raziel bandaging his arm, pulling the dressing tight to stop the bleeding underneath it. Why was Raziel still so gentle with him, despite him being such an idiot? Such a dependent, weak idiot.

"I'll help you take off your shirt, alright?" Raz said.

"No! Please..." Panic rose in Nate's voice.

Raz knew exactly how much he hated showing his back, and still he asked for it. Would he mark him, too? Now, that Nate thought he was safe with him? The phantom smell of smoke rushed into his nose once again, pushing his fears into overdrive.

"Nate, it's bloody," Raz explained. "If you want, I won't look, but you need to change, okay?"

The explanation barely arrived in his brain, so many more thoughts and doubts overshadowing it. If he could, he'd push Raziel away, but his body didn't move according to his commands.

"It's okay," the angel assured him. "You're safe with me. I promise, I'll never hurt you. I'd rather throw myself down a high-rise than bring you pain."

Very slowly, Nate looked at Raz, eyes wide open in panic. He was met by genuinely worried green eyes, Raz's forehead furrowed. Raz wouldn't hurt him, right? He could be trusted. Nate gulped and only reluctantly sat up with Raziel's help. The angel actually closed his eyes and helped him out of his shirt before dressing him in a fresh one. Nate's limbs were so slow and detached, almost as if they weren't even his, especially his left arm.

"Very good, Nate. Here, drink something."

Raz held a bottle of water out to Nate, who didn't even have the strength to protest. He just took some sips before he coughed. God, he was even too dumb to drink some plain water. It was embarrassing. But Raz just caressed his back and gently pushed him back onto the bed.

"I'll change and then I'll be with you," the angel promised.

Since their apartment was only one room, Nate could perfectly watch him undress down to his underwear, before Raz crawled into bed with him, pulling him onto his chest. Nate leaned his cheek against Raz's chest, his head still spinning and numb, but he felt a little better, despite what'd happened. Raziel's presence and warmth gave him comfort, and so had his words and the promises he'd made. Maybe this was Nate's lowest point? Maybe he would be better after this? One could only hope.

"You make everything okay," he whispered and just a second later, Raziel's fingers ran through his hair, calming him even more. Slowly, his consciousness delved into sweet and much needed sleep.

"I'll always save you from your demons," were the last whispered words he heard.

Maybe he needed a savior to heal his pain after all. He couldn't fight this on his own forever.

<h1 style="text-align:center">Chapter Fifteen
Broken Brain</h1>

OCTOBER 17TH, 2023

The tiredness and numbness didn't subside, not even the next day, despite sleeping for several hours while Raziel held Nate. His brain was still mushy, and his limbs were both heavy and numb.

"Nate...have you ever thought about therapy?" Raz carefully asked while they sat on the couch, eating breakfast. Raziel had prepared some cereal with milk, made a cup of tea, and even cut an apple for him.

Nate just shrugged and nibbled on a piece of apple. He wasn't hungry at all, but he knew he should eat a little, or his stomach would hurt later. He didn't want to disappoint Raz again either.

"It's too expensive," he mumbled.

The whole health system in the US was fucked up, and he knew he couldn't pay for therapy, not while also paying for rent and food, especially not in these times. Also, finding a therapist was hard. It took a lot of time and energy—energy Nate didn't have. Stumbling through life had already drained so much of his strength. How was he supposed to deal with finding a therapist, too?

Raziel placed the spoon in the bowl and turned to him. "Have you thought about Jamie's offer? To move in with him? We have double income, and we'd pay less rent. We could afford therapy for you then." His smile was soft, but his eyes were full of concern.

"I may be able to help you with the aftermath and the symptoms, but I'm no professional. I can't help you with the actual reasons for your depression."

Of course, Nate knew that, and even helping him through the bad days was too much to ask. His gaze wandered to his bandaged arm, a reminder of how much he had fucked up last night—how much of a burden he was to Raziel.

"I...haven't. But...it makes sense. I'll talk to him."

Nate still wasn't sure about this arrangement, about not having his own space anymore. But really, would it be so different? Right now, he didn't have his own space either, and not being alone felt good, it helped him, so maybe it wasn't the worst idea. They would still have their own room, and Jamie's place even had a living room, so they could spend time apart if they needed to.

Raziel leaned back, staring at the ceiling. He looked exhausted, too, and Nate was sorry he had to endure all this. If Raz wasn't dependent on living with him, he would certainly leave, right? Who would stay here with the mess he was and deal with him every single day? No one in their right mind would.

"Good." Raz gave a decisive nod. "I'll work your shift today, and you talk to Jamie. But you're coming to work with me. I won't leave you alone again."

Worried green eyes met his, Raz's gaze so intense that Nate had to look away. He stared at his only half-way empty bowl of cereal instead. It was reasonable, of course, no matter how much Nate felt like a little kid needing parental supervision. Raziel wasn't wrong. If he went into a bad headspace again, Raz could at least pull him out before he was in too deep.

He just wished he could be normal so no one had to worry about him.

HE WAS GLAD RAZ had taken his shift today since Nate could barely stand or walk. The world was spinning, and his hearing was muffled. Dark bags under his eyes showed how badly he had slept the last two nights. The bandage around his arm was hidden underneath a thin, long-sleeved shirt, so his coworkers wouldn't see it.

He texted Jamie to let him know to meet him at the cinema later. Meanwhile, he sipped his black tea and tried to concentrate on the book he'd brought to distract himself, but the words blurred before his eyes, and he understood barely anything.

Nate was relieved when he heard Jamie's voice from the door, calling his name, and immediately Nate answered that he was upstairs. It wasn't the first time Jamie had been in their break room, and he knew where to go.

"Hey! Shit, Nate, you look like shit. What happened?"

Jamie sat down next to him with a worried expression, and Nate put away the book. This would be an intense talk. He didn't want to tell Jamie everything—not here, not now—just some basic information.

"Daniel was at my door two days ago," Nate began. "He and Raz got into a fight, and he lost, but...I'm scared he'll be back and do worse."

He had never told Jamie how bad his relationship had actually been and what Daniel had done to him. He wouldn't now, either. Maybe someday, but he wasn't quite ready yet.

"I need therapy," he continued. "And Raz reminded me that you asked me to move in with you. That offer still open?"

Shit, he hadn't kept up with Jamie's living situation at all. Maybe he'd found an apartment on his own already and they'd need to figure out a different solution.

Jamie's eyes lit up. "Sure! Alex is moving out this weekend. I still can't find an apartment, and I started searching for a roommate, but I really don't want a stranger around me at all times."

"Thanks, man," Nate said.

"Oh, and of course the offer's for you and Raziel both. We can go through the details later." Jamie leaned toward him, worried, and a question in his brown eyes. "But what's going on with you? Why therapy? I mean, it's a good thing!"

Nate sighed. It had been so unfair to hide all his struggles from Jamie, to keep it all inside out of fear of annoying him. Jamie was his best friend; if he could talk to anyone it was him. Yet Nate hadn't wanted to burden his friend with all his problems, nor had he wanted to accept how lost and broken he actually was, how much he hurt inside.

"I...I'm depressed," he admitted. "And it's not getting better. I'm drinking too much, eating too little, and..." For a moment he struggled but then pushed up his sleeve a little so Jamie could see the bandage before hiding it again. He couldn't say what had happened, but he hoped Jamie understood anyway.

Just a moment later, Jamie's arms wrapped around him, and he was pulled into a hug. The comforting warmth and soft pressure of Jamie's squeeze reassured him that he wasn't alone. Nate had needed this so much.

"I'm here," Jamie promised, "if you want to talk or if I can help you in any way. It's good you're moving in with me, then you'll be even less alone. And you'll have kitties around you all the time."

Jamie smiled at him, and Nate smiled back, though it was a tired smile. He was just so exhausted that even this small talk had drained his energy. How had he dealt with all this on his own for so long? It wasn't surprising that he was on the edge, barely holding on.

"Raziel knows about all this?" Jamie asked.

Nate just nodded. Of course, the angel knew; he couldn't hide anything from him, not while they were living together in a one-room apartment—not when it was Raziel who'd found him, unconscious and bleeding.

"Therapy's a good idea," Jamie said. "It'll help you. And I can help you find a therapist, too. I've heard it's annoying and exhausting, and you're in no state to go through this on your own."

Jamie's offer was a huge relief. He was sure it'd be impossible to find a therapist on his own, and he was incredibly glad his best friend was at his side.

"Thanks. I'm glad to have you," Nate said, and a tiny smile tugged on his lips.

The fact that Jamie now knew what was going on made things easier. To know he'd support Nate at all times, even in the darkest ones, comforted Nate and pushed his dark thoughts away for the moment.

But still, love alone was not enough. Love was no magical cure for a broken brain. It was time to get the help he so desperately needed.

CHAPTER SIXTEEN

The Truth Was Revealed

OCTOBER 29TH, 2023

Moving happened quite fast, since the room in Jamie's apartment was already free. Luckily, there hadn't been too much to pack either; Nate had never owned many things, and with Raziel's and Jamie's help, everything had been in boxes quickly. Nate couldn't wait to decorate their new room, to feel at home again, a home with Raziel by his side. The idea alone sent butterflies through his stomach and made his heart beat quicker.

It was exhilarating to be free of the oppressive memories the apartment had left in Nate. It was connected to Daniel, to so many bad things happening to him, and a fresh start was exactly what he needed.

The relief that Daniel wouldn't know where he lived anymore was yet another pleasant side effect. His ex couldn't just wait in front of his door. Nate wouldn't be surprised if Daniel decided to take revenge on him—and Raziel—if he caught them again. The man wasn't a stranger to violence and threats. By now, Nate wouldn't put it past Daniel to resort to worse ways to deal with them.

But today was a good day, and Nate wanted to concentrate on it. They were finally in their new home, helped by some coworkers, who moved all the furniture and boxes, so everything went pretty quickly. Though there was more work to be done, they threw a little welcome party after they had at least assembled the bed. Nate wished he had more money to buy a new one, as well as a new mattress; this furniture held bad associations. But it held good ones, too, like the times he had cuddled with Raziel, or when they had slept with each other the first—and only—time.

Although Nate wanted to sleep with his boyfriend again, Raz had asked him to get an STD test before, and Nate had agreed. It made sense because Daniel had never used a condom when he slept around. It wouldn't be surprising if that asshole had contagious diseases.

For now, Nate didn't want to think about his ex but, rather, focused on the moment.

Jamie had ordered some pizza for everyone, and they had some cases of beer, as well, for their helpers and themselves. Despite his exhaustion, Nate was relieved they had actually done this and gone through with the move.

He sat next to Raziel on the couch, leaning comfortably against the angel. He was already drunk despite only having had some beers, but he hadn't eaten much again, so that was unsurprising. Neither Raz nor Jamie had caught up with that yet.

"You can go to sleep already," Raz mumbled into his ear, an arm around Nate's shoulder, holding him close. But Nate only shook his head slightly. He didn't want to sleep yet, not at their housewarming.

Raz sighed but nodded and ran his fingers through Nate's blue hair while taking a sip from his own can of beer. So much for being an angel. Nate chuckled a little, since it was such a fun thought to him right now. An angel who drank and fucked and got pierced. What a contradiction.

He didn't listen to the conversation the others were having, just sipped more of his own beer. His guts churned, and he realized he was going to be sick. A bit uncoordinated, Nate got up and stumbled out of the living room to the bathroom, where he closed the door behind him and kneeled in front of the toilet. At least he managed that before his stomach convulsed, ejecting all the alcohol he'd drunk and the two slices of pizza he'd eaten.

It was frustrating, his body working against him, but it might be all the stress from moving and being up all day. It had been exhausting to carry all the boxes and furniture out of his old apartment and into their new room. Even with their helpers, it had taken the whole day. Sleep might not be the worst idea in the end.

When he finally felt a little better, Nate got up and washed his face, also rinsing out his mouth. Not how he had planned to celebrate their housewarming. When he opened the door again, he was greeted by Raziel waiting for him, one eyebrow raised.

"Time for bed, huh?" Raz said. "Come on, it's fine. I got you some water, and sleep will be good for you."

Nate didn't protest when Raziel gently led him toward their new room and their bed. Nate sank down on the bed and allowed his boyfriend to help him get rid of his pants and be placed underneath the blanket.

"Don't worry about it, alright? Just get some rest, I'll be with you later," Raziel promised and kissed his cheek before he left the room with a loving smile.

And for once, Nate actually fell asleep easily and even slept through the night, even when Raziel came into bed and cuddled close up to him.

OCTOBER 30TH, 2023

Nate woke up because the sun was shining into their room. Right, they hadn't hung their curtains yet. Yawning, he got up slowly and stretched, remembering the night before. At least he felt better today.

He looked over at Raziel, who mumbled something incomprehensible and turned around, now facing the wall. Adorable. A smile tugged on Nate's lips as he gazed at the angel, and he wondered how late he'd stayed up last night.

Silently, Nate left the room and closed the door behind him so Raz could sleep some more. When he entered the living room, he was greeted by the smell of beer and cold pizza. It almost made him nauseous again, and he decided he had to clean up the mess left over from last night. Nate was glad no one had stayed overnight, and it was just Jamie, Raz, and him. Well, and of course the cats, the tabby one roaming around his legs, purring.

To give the kitty some attention, Nate leaned down and scratched her behind her ears for a moment. Her fur was so soft and warm, a welcome sensation underneath his fingers. Another wave of cold-pizza-and-beer-smell reminded him of the mess in the living room. Right, he wanted to clean.

All the leftover pizza slices fit into one box, which Nate put aside, and all opened but unfinished beer cans were drained before Nate threw them into the trash. He also wiped the small table he and Raziel had brought from their old apartment. Nate was glad they had brought some things, like the sofa. They just had to buy a new fridge, since Alex had taken the one in this apartment, leaving Jamie without a fridge for over two weeks. She had also taken the modem, making Jamie's search for a new apartment even harder. Really a weird person, and if Nate hadn't thought she was a bad friend already, now he was sure about it from her immature behavior

"Ah, you're already awake," Jamie said. "Good morning."

Jamie was scuffling into the kitchen, his dark hair standing up at all sides, a tired smile on his face. He grabbed a box from the kitchen drawer and filled the cats' bowls with kibble. Immediately, two very happy cats munched away, and Nate just watched them for a moment.

"You sleep okay?" Nate asked, smiling at him. "It's probably weird not having the apartment to yourself anymore."

Jamie just shrugged and yawned. "Could've been worse. Bastet woke me up jumping around and knocking stuff off shelves."

Typical cat behavior, then, especially from an orange cat. So far, the cats hadn't been in his and Raziel's room, and they still had to decide if they wanted to let them in. Nate knew Alex hadn't allowed them inside, and if they got used to it, it would be annoying to always have their door open. Especially if they wanted some privacy. On the other hand, cats around were always a great thing. Their purring and warm little bodies were soothing.

"Good thing I got a free day," Jamie said. "I can help you with the furniture." He smiled sheepishly. "Though, I kinda need to wake up first,"

Nate chuckled and was quite glad to have Jamie. They didn't really have much furniture, but it would still be helpful to have a third pair of hands around. He would also have to secure the hooks for his guitars so he could put them back on a wall. They deserved some more attention, after he'd neglected them for months. Nate was completely out of practice, with no motivation to play. It was just another side effect of being depressed, and it sucked.

Together, they headed into the living room, where Jamie grabbed a pack of cigarettes from the table and went toward the balcony door. Nate instinctively recoiled. He didn't know Jamie smoked, aside from one here and there when he was drunk at parties.

"Want one, too?" Jamie offered, turning to him.

Immediately, Nate shook his head and curled up more on the sofa, glad to feel a small, furry animal next to him to distract him.

For a long time, he watched Jamie smoke outside and was glad he'd closed the door behind him so Nate didn't smell the smoke—at least until Jamie came back inside, one last cloud of smoke following him.

As soon as the smell hit his nose, Nate's body felt numb again, and he put his arms around his knees, making himself as small as possible. His hands started shaking, and he clawed his fingers into the skin of his thighs. The small pain did little to distract him. Fuck, why did he react so much to this? It wasn't logical. Jamie wasn't the first person to smoke around him besides Daniel, but neither his brain nor his body were functioning logically right now.

Memories started rising up of Daniel grinning at him while he flicked on his lighter. His whole body hurt, tensed up entirely, and panic rushed through him. It couldn't happen again; Nate couldn't bear that torture once more.

"Nate? What's wrong? Are you sick again?"

A hand touched his shoulder, and his body jerked away before he stared up at his best friend. Jamie's face was just a blur, his voice muffled and mixing with the static in Nate's ears. He couldn't speak, and his mind was looping memories: Daniel's hands on his body, no matter if Nate wanted them or not; his father yelling before he hit a much younger Nate; a firm grasp around his neck, choking him. Nate's breath got faster and shallower, and it got harder to breathe. He felt like he was suffocating once again.

Nate barely noticed he was mumbling, pleading with his abusers not to hurt him again. He only thought of the inevitable pain to come, preparing for the heat that surely would meet his skin in a moment, scorching it and leaving yet another mark.

Only when he was shaken by the shoulders did his sight clear up slowly, and Nate heard the voice that had been a muffled mumbling.

"Sh, it's okay. It's Jamie, not Daniel. Look at me, Nate."

Nate's vision cleared up more, but it took another moment to understand that Raz was kneeling in front of him. The angel's hands wandered from his shoulders to his cheeks and forced him to look right into those dark green eyes. Breath after breath, Nate calmed down, distracted from his destructive memories. Deflated, he sank forward and leaned his head against Raziel's shoulder, a choking sob escaping him.

There was so much pain inside him, more than Nate had ever known existed. Or, really, he hadn't been able to admit the extent to which he was broken.

Raziel's arms were around his back, holding him gently, and his closeness and the scent of citrus, myrrh, and even a little pizza from last night reminded Nate he was safe. Raziel wouldn't hurt him—the angel had promised.

"Jamie deserves to know." Raz's lips were right next to his ear, whispering to him, so Jamie couldn't hear. "He can't help you if he doesn't know."

Nate's thoughts were still slow, not quite back in the present, and he wasn't sure if it was a good idea, either. Was he actually ready to reveal one of his biggest shames, what had been done to him for so many years?

But in the end, Raziel was right. Jamie deserved to know—and so did Raziel himself.

Nate took a deep breath and sat up a little straighter. His hands still shook, but he managed to look at Jamie, who was standing close to the couch. His best friend clearly was unsure what to do and worried about what had just happened.

"I...it's easier to show you," Nate mumbled.

With numb fingers, he pulled up his shirt and got rid of it. It was uncomfortable to be shirtless in front of others; it was already hard enough to undress when he was by himself. But the time to trust the people he loved had come. Nate gathered all his courage to turn his back to Jamie, giving him a full view of all the little scars strewn across his shoulders and upper back, some almost faded, some just a few months old.

"Whenever my father was angry, he punished me by putting out a cigarette on my back," Nate tearfully explained. "Daniel found out and did the same after—"

Nate gulped, not ready to say it yet. It hadn't been consensual sex. He realized that, but had it really been rape? Nate's brain still fought against the idea of it, and he certainly wouldn't say it aloud. It would make things too real. Running from reality and trauma was a much easier way to deal with things than confronting them.

"Nate…"

It was just a whisper, but Jamie sounded shocked and at a loss for words. Afraid of Jamie's and Raz's reactions, Nate turned back around. Would they be disgusted? Or disappointed that he was such a mess? But Raz was still kneeling in front of him, his green eyes so warm and worried that it made Nate tear up.

Jamie kneeled down next to Raz and gingerly took Nate's hand. "I'm so sorry I triggered memories." There was no disgust or disappointment on his face, just genuine worry and love. "I won't do it again. Your father and ex deserve to burn in hell for what they did to you."

Nate wasn't sure what to say, and he wasn't sure if he would even be able to. There was a lump in his throat, and tears were flowing down his cheeks. Both men hugged him and held him close, no one saying anything. They held him as he cried, finally releasing some of the pain and sorrow he had stuffed down for so long.

The truth was revealed, and he still had the two guys he loved most by his side.

CHAPTER SEVENTEEN

NOVEMBER 2ND, 2023

Only a few days after Nate revealed his scars, he and Jamie started looking for therapists. It was even harder than Nate had imagined. They had to search through endless websites, most which wanted you to call the office and not just send an email.

The little energy Nate had every day was drained by the search, and after two fruitless calls, he was close to giving up. Getting rejected hurt, as if his pain wasn't valid or not enough to deserve help.

Curled up on the couch, Nate stared at the ton of tabs he had open on Jamie's laptop. How was he supposed to find help when he had no spoons to do so? How did people find a therapist at all?

He only looked up when Jamie came back into the living room and plopped down next to him, legs crossed and the laptop on his lap. Baby followed him and jumped up on the couch as well, curling up next to Nate. His hand wandered to the soft tabby fur, the vibrations underneath his fingers relaxing him just a little.

"That's another old guy," Jamie complained and closed another tab. "Why are so many therapists old white guys? How annoying."

It had been Jamie's suggestion to look for a younger therapist, someone who wouldn't be so closed minded, especially considering Nate was gay. Nate had no intention of talking to someone who reminded him of his father—too many bad memories.

"I'm sorry I need your help with this," he whispered.

If he just had more energy, more motivation, he wouldn't have to rely on Jamie helping him or on Raziel taking yet another one of his shifts. His boyfriend had offered to work for him today so Nate and Jamie had time to concentrate on finding a therapist.

"Nate, it's alright," Jamie assured him. "I offered you my help, and I support you, always. We'll find someone. Don't apologize. You're not well, and it's normal to need help then."

Jamie smiled at him before his attention shifted back to the screen. How grateful Nate was to have such a wonderful best friend who supported him without any hesitation and without Nate even asking him for help.

A bit absentmindedly, Nate's fingertips traced the red lines on his forearm. Two and a half weeks had passed since that fateful night, since he'd almost ended all his struggles and suffering. Although some things had changed already—mainly moving in with Jamie and out of Daniel's reach—his thoughts hadn't changed much.

Nate was convinced he was a burden. Jamie sacrificing his free day to look through endless therapist sites and Raziel working six days a week were proof enough for that.

"Oooh! Let's try this one!" Jamie said excitedly. "It doesn't say she won't take new patients, *and* she's younger."

As Jamie started typing a number into his phone, Nate's brow furrowed. He knew how much Jamie hated phone calls, as much as he did—and still Jamie called every single therapist he thought could be a good fit.

"Yes, hi! This is Jamie Koskinen. I'm calling for my friend Nathaniel."

Nate glanced at his best friend, who was now listening intently to the voice on the other side.

"I understand that," Jamie said. "He's sitting next to me. I can put you on speaker. He's not in the right state to call on his own."

It was weird to have Jamie talk about him, but Nate appreciated his help.

Jamie put the call on speaker and held the phone in his hand so they both could hear the feminine voice.

"*I'm sure you're a great friend,*" she said. "*But I can't give out more information to non-relatives.*"

The same as every time Jamie had called. It was frustrating, and Nate wondered how people even found a therapist. This fucked up health system would rather see them dead than get help.

Swallowing hard, Nate took a deep, shaky breath. "H-hi, I'm Na-Nathaniel Lachner. Jamie called for me. I—" He had no idea what to say exactly. "I'm looking for therapy, as I'm probably depressed and have PTSD."

At least that's what Nate guessed. It was pretty clear to him, after his reaction to Jamie smoking. It wasn't just depression; there was more to it than that, and it was disrupting his life too much to ignore.

"*Mr. Lachner, let me please check my appointment book.*" It was silent for a moment; only the soft rustle of paper could be heard. "*Are you able to come in for an initial interview on Monday at 3pm?*"

Surprised that he'd gotten so lucky, Nate glanced at Jamie, who smiled broadly and nodded to him. It reassured Nate this was really happening—he had an offer for a first appointment.

"Yes! I can be there."

His fingers clawed into his pants, as if he was trying to remind himself this was real. He would actually be able to talk to a therapist and would hopefully secure himself a permanent one.

"Then I'll add your name to the calendar. If you have prior paperwork or diagnoses, please bring them to the appointment. I recommend you come in ten minutes early, so you can fill out the paperwork without stress. The initial interview will take about two hours in most cases. Do you have further questions?"

It was a lot of information already, and Nate's head was buzzing. But all he said was, "I don't think so. Thank you!"

Was it silly to thank a therapist for an initial interview? Maybe, but the relief that flooded Nate was immense. His hands were shaking, and his whole body shivered. He barely noticed Jamie ending the call, could only stare straight at the table in front of them.

He would actually get help, professional help. Now he only had to hope it wouldn't just be an initial interview, but the therapist had a spot open for regular sessions—and wasn't too expensive.

NOVEMBER 17TH, 2023

Nate had barely been so nervous about anything before. Although he'd gotten through the initial evaluation—in which his new therapist had confirmed he was very much depressed and most likely had C-PTSD as well—the first real appointment felt different.

The office only had a small waiting room with two chairs, which were both occupied—one by Nate and the other by Raz, who had taken it upon himself to accompany Nate to the appointment.

The angel got up and hunkered down right in front of Nate. Warm hands grabbed Nate's shaking ones, and his attention shifted to the beautiful green eyes looking up at him. There was so much warmth and love radiating from Raz that it calmed Nate's rapid heartbeat.

"It's gonna be okay, Nate," Raz promised. "You told me you'll go through your biography today, right?"

Nate gave a small nod, and his fingers curled up around Raz's hands. He was incredibly glad to not be alone and that Raz would also pick him up after the session. Jamie and Raz would make sure he'd attend all sessions and didn't run from it, no matter how painful it would be.

"My biography is such a mess, though," Nate mumbled and managed a crooked smile.

If it wasn't, he surely wouldn't be here needing therapy. It sucked, but he wanted to be better, wanted to enjoy life and be a good friend and boyfriend. He deserved happiness in his life.

So far, he hadn't told Raz much about his past or how he grew up because Nate just didn't want to think about it. It would be painful to do so, but there was no way around it, no matter how much he dreaded it.

Before Raz could say anything, a feminine voice disrupted them. "Mr. Lachner?"

His therapist, Miss Fraser, was a young woman in her late 20s or early 30s, with straight black hair pulled back into a ponytail and round glasses on her nose. She gave Nate some big sister vibes, about the same height as him but plumper.

"Yes, I'm coming." Nate leaned down to his boyfriend and gave him a soft kiss before he got up. He'd see Raz after his appointment, could hug him again, and he was rather sure he'd need it.

Nervously, he followed the therapist back to her office, hesitating before stepping over the threshold. She offered him a seat and took one of her own, and though her voice was gentle and inviting, Nate still felt nauseous.

Settled on a plush armchair, Nate forced himself to sit up straight instead of curling into himself the way he wanted to. The velvety texture of the dark green chair underneath his fingers distracted him a bit, as did the many plants in the office. It was easier to look at those than to look at Miss Fraser.

"As I told you the last time," she said, "we'll start with your biography. It normally takes two sessions, and then we can start diving into your struggles. How are you feeling today?"

Her voice was warm and soft, and there was thankfully no pity. Nate would've hated that. He didn't want any pity; he wanted to work on his issues.

"I'm nervous," he admitted. "Anxious even. If my boyfriend hadn't accompanied me, I might not have entered the building."

That was a big enough admission for him already, and he was so afraid of diving into his own mind and psyche. For so many years, Nate had been used to running from it, distracting himself from it, using unhealthy coping mechanisms. Now that he was here, he didn't really know that he could do this.

Miss Fraser nodded and gave him a small smile. "It's completely normal to be afraid and nervous of therapy. It will unravel a lot in you, but you won't go through this alone." She walked over to her desk to pull out a box, which she set down on the table in front of him. Nate spotted many little trinkets inside, from spiky balls—some metal, others rubber or plastic—to little metal rings that looked like springs, vials of oil, and even a fidget spinner. "You can use one of these to calm yourself a little. We'll talk about the use of skills more when the time's right."

Curiously, Nate leaned forward and scanned the box's contents. There was one purple metal spiky ball that caught his attention, and he grabbed it before leaning back again. The slight pressure and pain of the spikes pressing into his palms helped him focus a bit more, and he relaxed a little.

"Are you okay to start?" Miss Fraser asked, and after a glance at her, Nate nodded. "How did you grow up as a child?" was the first question.

The memories brought up mixed emotions in Nate. On the one hand, those were the few good memories he had of his family, but on the other hand, his childhood had ended too early, with a tragic accident.

"I was born in Germany—Eastern Germany to be precise. Grew up with my parents in a big house. They didn't marry out of love but just because I was conceived."

It was a fact Nate had learned about quite early; his father had made no secret out of it.

"How was your relationship with your parents?" Miss Fraser asked.

Warmth flooded Nate as he thought of his mother. "My mom was wonderful. She was always sweet with me. We did a lot of puzzles and read together. She even took me to riding classes. My father wasn't very invested. We played some soccer sometimes, but he was working a lot and cared more about my grades and what other people thought about the family than emotions."

Which had never changed of course. But they'd surely get to this later. Nate's attention was fixed on the big monstera, with its lush, green leaves, on the windowsill next to him.

"Were there other important people in your childhood?" she asked. "Siblings, grandparents, parental figures?"

There weren't many people who had cared about Nate in general, but one had been there—and Nate had to set up a facetime call soon. He had neglected doing so for too long.

"My grandma," he said. "My father's mother. She picked me up after school, cooked for me, and was always there when my parents were working. I haven't seen her since I moved to the States."

It brought up even more guilt, as he should have visited his grandma at least once, but plane tickets from the US to Germany were just too expensive. Not to mention his dwindling mental health hadn't allowed him to save money or plan a trip.

When she asked about school, that was quite easy to talk about. At first. Nate had never had many friends, and he'd often been the best in his classes, especially in reading and writing. It had gained him his father's praise, but not his love. As he thought about all of that now, it made him sick, reminded him how much he'd changed and how dumb he'd become.

"How did your relationship with your parents change when you grew up?" Miss Fraser asked.

Nate squeezed the metal ball in his hand, the blunt spikes pressing deep into his palm. "My mother died in a car accident when I was eight. I was devastated, and I still miss her a lot. My father blamed me because I was in the car with her. I distracted her, reading with the light on in the backseat."

Tears threatened to bubble up, and Nate squeezed the ball even harder. Even after so many years, it still hurt, and it had been the end of a happy childhood for him.

"My father got to know an American woman two years later and started ignoring or hitting me for everything I did wrong. A bad grade at school, playing with my toys too loud, not helping with the garden—it didn't matter."

His thumb brushed over the spikes, pressed into the texture, but Nate barely noticed it left some red marks. It hurt so much less than what he'd had to endure.

"We moved to Florida when I was twelve," he said, sniffling. "I barely spoke English, and I was always the freak in school from then on. My grades got worse, and I was close to failing almost every class. That's when he started to..." Nate swallowed, unable to keep the tears back anymore. They ran over his cheeks and dropped onto his hands. "When he started to burn me with cigarettes."

It was just a whisper, barely audible, even to himself. The scars itched underneath his hoodie, burned as if they were fresh, and Nate could almost smell the cold smoke and burned flesh. His own younger self's screams echoed in his mind, making his ears ring. Nate could barely breathe, bent over and gasping for air.

He flinched when his shoulders were touched, but only saw Miss Fraser's round face in front of him, her warm brown eyes covered by glasses. "It's okay," she promised. "You're not alone. Breathe, slowly. Count with me."

Nate followed her guidance, at first with a lot of trouble, but his breath calmed down and so did his heartbeat. Miss Fraser retreated to her armchair and offered him a box of tissues. Although Nate had known therapy would be painful, he hadn't expected to have a full-on panic attack during the first session.

After blowing his nose and wiping his face, he took a deep breath and pressed the metal spikes into his palm once more, to remind himself he wasn't in his father's house anymore, but free and safe.

"Are you alright to continue?" she asked. "We can end the session, if you'd like to."

The therapist's offer was tempting, but Nate knew he wouldn't get through this again if he stopped now. He had to face his fears, had to work through the painful memories.

"I'm okay. Not my first panic attack." A crooked smile curled on his lips but disappeared just a moment later. "I have two half-siblings. They're thirteen and fourteen years younger than me. My father treated them like royalty."

While Nate himself had been abused and punished for every single thing he did, no matter how hard he tried. The unfairness still roused anger and resentment in him that made his blood boil.

"When he figured out I was gay," Nate continued, swallowing down the lump in his throat, "he threw me out for good. I was seventeen at the time. I dropped out of school and had no idea where to go. I had online friends on the West Coast, and my grandma sent me money for a plane ticket. I've had no contact with my father ever since, and I don't want it either."

To Nate, that man was dead. He'd been lucky to have friends with a place for him to sleep and that his grandma had accepted and supported him. Still did, even now that he only called irregularly. Without her support as an anchor, Nate surely would've ended up either in a ditch or as an addict.

His hands were still damp, and his stomach was tight, but he was relieved to have managed to get his whole rough, messy life story out in the open. Only Jamie knew most of it, but aside from him, no other friends did. There was just too much pain connected to his family and lost youth—a youth Nate had never been allowed to fully enjoy.

When she realized he was finished, Miss Fraser smiled at him again. "Thank you for sharing, Nate."

He didn't know what to say. "You're welcome" was most appropriate, but it felt weird. "I'm sorry you had to hear it" was probably *not* the right way to go, but it was closest to what he said. Eventually, though, he settled on, "Thank you for listening."

And then he started crying again.

Family Matters

DECEMBER 3RD, 2023

Being in therapy was exhausting, but also relieving. Nate had had three sessions so far and they had only scratched on the surface of his trauma and his problems. But just talking about all the shit that had happened to him, having someone who didn't judge him but just listened to what he was saying, was so helpful, and Nate was certainly glad it'd worked out nicely so far.

His therapist hadn't put him on meds yet. They talked about them, but they'd both agreed that for now he should try going without. If he realized his mood hadn't changed at all, they were going to revisit the option.

That evening after a quick nap at home after therapy, he set up his tablet in the living room. Jamie was working late, and Raziel was probably on his way home from work. Nate wanted to call his grandma, and this was the perfect opportunity. The last time had been some weeks ago and was only a quick chat via phone, so he was glad she'd agreed to video chat today. He missed seeing her.

His grandma always needed a heads up for that to set up her own tablet, which she'd gotten just for this purpose. His uncle had helped her set everything up and was also around today in case any technical issues arose.

As soon as Nate saw the old woman on his tablet, a smile spread across his face. She was the one person in his family that actually cared about him, and he was damn sad he hadn't been able to visit her for over ten years. Therapy had at least given him enough energy to start the regular calls again.

"Hallo, Oma. Schön dich zu sehen."

"Nathan! Ich hab mir schon Sorgen gemacht!"

Of course, she had been worried, and Nate was so sorry about that, but she didn't know a lot about what'd been going on with him. He could never bring himself to say anything. It was time to tell her about therapy, at least, and that he had moved. Next to him, Baby purred and stretched her furry head a little, appearing on his video as well.

He barely registered how fast time went by while talking to his grandma, and only when he heard the door being unlocked did he look up for a moment. That should be Raz coming home.

"Hey, kitty, I'm home!" Raz called. "Where are you?"

Nate chuckled and called for Raziel, only to see him just a moment later, still occupied with unwrapping the scarf around his neck and taking off his hat. It'd gotten cold, and even an angel needed protection from this weather.

When Raziel leaned down to Nate, he spotted the tablet and video call. An awkward smile set on Raziel's lips, but he didn't retreat. It filled Nate's heart with joy to have this man at his side, to have his support, and that he didn't run from meeting Nate's grandma.

"Oh, hi!" Raz said, still a little awkward.

"That's my grandma," Nate explained softly, knowing very well his grandma understood absolutely no word of what they were saying, since she didn't speak any English.

"How do you say 'hello' in German?" Raz asked whispering.

"It's 'hallo.'"

And without hesitation, Raziel greeted his grandma. His pronunciation was a bit off. but the gesture was adorable.

"I'll leave you to it." Raz smiled at him and pressed a kiss on his temple, making him blush, before he left the living room again.

"Wer ist denn dieser junge Mann?" his grandma immediately interrogated him.

Good thing she knew he was gay and had never had a problem with it; it meant he could explain to her that was his boyfriend. Given his past experiences with men, it was still incredible to Nate that he could call someone his boyfriend and feel proud of it.

They talked about all sorts of things, and his grandma left him with a lot of things to consider, including asking him to come to Germany to see her. After a promise to call her again next week to inform her of his decision, the call ended. Nate leaned back and closed his eyes for a moment, still smiling. This talk had been good, despite the heavy topics, and it was nice to remember there was at least one person in his family who actually cared about him, which Nate regularly doubted.

"You okay?" he heard Raz's voice from the doorway.

Nate's attention shifted to the angel, who leaned against the doorway and looked him. Raziel had changed out of his regular work clothes into his sweatpants and a slightly cat-hair-infested shirt. Nate loved this casual look.

"Mmmhmm, just a lot to think about."

His boyfriend nodded and came closer, one hand against the backrest of the couch, leaning down to press their lips together. Their kisses became more and more intense as his other hand found its way underneath Nate's shirt. What was his plan? Well, dumb question—he could guess what Raz's plan was, and Nate didn't mind at all.

He pulled Raziel closer, gliding his fingers over his flat stomach and deepening the kiss. He loved this intimacy, these little moments between them where he didn't have to worry if Raz was going to hurt him. Nate trusted him fully, and it didn't matter they'd only known each other for a few months. Trust was earned, and so far, Raz hadn't given him any reason not to trust.

Nate watched in awe as the angel kneeled down between his legs, pushing his shirt up a little. Warm lips pressed kisses to his stomach, eliciting a soft sigh from Nate. His own fingers wandered into Raziel's long hair, just stroking it a little, letting Raz do whatever he wanted.

As soon as he felt the hand in his pants, he knew what was up and chuckled slightly. Distraction from his long talk, huh? He wouldn't complain, and neither would his body. It was so easy for Raz to get him going, despite Nate having struggled so much with enjoying any kind of intimacy for the last few years—even on his own. With Raz, he reacted very sensitively to every single one of the angel's touches and kisses.

Soon, his pants were pulled down a little, exposing his hardening middle. Soft lips cupped him, sent hot shivers through his body, and Nate couldn't hold back a low moan.

The angel's lip piercing was still unusual when kissing or in such situations, but it made the whole experience even more special and unique. Like most times, it didn't take long for Nate to come. Full of fondness and satisfaction, his fingers grabbed the light hair a little firmer while he enjoyed the sight.

Raz licked his lips and grinned at him—a view that made Nate long for more. For now, he only got a soft kiss.

"You up for a hot bath and telling me what you're thinking about?" the angel suggested, now in a completely innocent tone of voice. This guy...

"If I get more of you, sure."

His words made Raziel laugh, and he was pulled up, adjusting his pants so he could walk better to the bathroom, where he would lose them anyway.

While Raz turned on the faucet, Nate took off his clothes. It was still awkward for him to be completely naked in front of others, and he could only do this with Raziel. They were both scarred, and it made it easier for Nate.

Raz was the first one to enter the tub after he put his hair in a bun, so it wouldn't get wet, before Nate followed. It wasn't the first time they'd done this, and Nate took his place between Raz's legs and cuddled against his chest. As soon as he sat, Raz's arms wrapped around him, and he was held tenderly. Raz's lips pressed against his shoulder as he kissed one scar after the other. It had become kind of a ritual for Raziel to kiss his scars, to acknowledge the pain and memories this way instead of ignoring them or treating them as something to be ashamed of.

The angel also gingerly grabbed his left arm and ran his thumb over the scars there several times, saying, "It's healing well."

Nate just nodded. The cuts really were healing well, and the superficial ones were barely visible anymore. Only the bigger one was still a red line, and he was sure it would stay a scar forever, only fading but never disappearing. Neither would his other scars. They could fade but never leave him completely.

"What's going on in your mind?" Raz asked. "What did your grandma ask you to think about?"

Nate closed his eyes and leaned against his boyfriend more, his hands on Raz's arms, holding onto him a little. The support and reassurance of Raz's closeness was something Nate needed.

"She wants me to visit her," Nate explained. "I told her I'd love to, but it's too expensive, especially with therapy now. Flights are, like, $550 each way. She insisted and said she'd pay for the travel, and I could stay at her house. Like, her pension isn't too bad, but I still don't want to use her money."

Raz hummed quietly, a sign he was thinking. It always gave Nate a little reassurance that he wasn't being ignored, that he'd get an answer eventually, even if it took some time.

Finally, Raz nodded. "You should go. She's what, like, eighty? Use the time while you can. You told me she really cares about you and loves you the way you are, right? It's hard to find family like that. Cherish every moment with her. I can't do that anymore because my family's dead, but you can."

Raz was right, of course he was. He should use the opportunity and visit her, especially after he hadn't seen her for half his life—wait, what did Raz say about his own family?

Nate turned around a little and looked at the angel, confused. "Your family's dead? I thought your family are other angels?"

Now there was confusion on Raz's face before he blinked and shook his head a little. Nate wasn't sure what was going on in Raziel's head, but something had gotten mixed up there. Or had he been lying the whole time? Made up the whole angel thing? But that didn't make sense either. Nate had met another angel, right? Hadn't he?

In the end, Nate didn't mind either option. He was okay if Raz had escaped some cult, or if he was an actual angel—it changed nothing about *who* he was, not to Nate.

"Yeah. Yeah, you're right," Raz said after a few more moments of silence. "It's getting confusing with my fake identity and reality. Still, you should go and visit your grandma."

Slowly, Nate nodded, still not convinced Raz was telling the truth. He would talk to his grandma next week and tell her, then try to find a good date to visit. Probably in January, since he wouldn't be able to get any paid time off before Christmas. It was too stressful to travel during Christmas time anyway.

But he certainly would keep an eye on Raz and what was going on with him. Was he adjusting too much? Or were his real memories coming back? Either of these things could be confusing and scrambling his brain.

Maybe some distraction would help for now.

Nate turned around completely, now sitting on Raz's lap, and initiated a heated kiss. After all, he had asked to get more of Raz, and the angel had agreed.

Chapter Nineteen

Nightmares

DECEMBER 13TH, 2023

With Christmas just around the corner, work was even busier, and neither Nate nor Raziel had much free time with all the long shifts they were working. But it wasn't too bad, at least they often worked the same ones, and they still had their nights and mornings together. Working more also meant more money, which they both desperately needed.

Christmas shopping this year would be pretty easy for Nate. Mostly. He was only getting presents for Raz, Jamie, and his grandma, so it wouldn't take that long. He'd already sent the present for his grandma, since it would take quite some time to arrive, and he knew what he wanted to get Jamie, but he was still struggling to find an idea what to gift Raziel.

"You're fine with staying here at Christmas?" he asked Raziel while they cuddled in bed, a movie playing in the background. The movie was less important than being close to Raz, cuddling underneath their blanket, cozy and warm.

"Hm? Sure, I have nowhere else to be anyway." Raz shrugged and stared at the monitor again. The angel's hand wandered to his temple and rubbed it, before he groaned and closed his eyes.

Nate looked at him in concern. "Headache again?"

Raz just nodded. These headaches had become a frequent occurrence lately, and neither of them knew where they were coming from. Nate had also noticed Raz was often just staring into the distance. It sucked to have no idea how to help or where these struggles were coming from.

"Christmas is such bullshit anyway," Raz said bitterly. "Celebrating some guy who was really charismatic but such a cult-leader. Y'know, the Bible and all that shit was just written down by normal people."

A bit surprised by the annoyed tone, Nate looked at his boyfriend, worried but also curious. Of course, Raz would know more about the origin of all these stories and beliefs. And while it surprised him to hear an angel talking so badly about the Bible, it sounded like it was justified. Nate had never cared much for religion anyway, not even now when he had a literal angel in his bed.

"So, it wasn't a miracle or some intervention from God?"

Raz just scoffed. "'Course not. Some guy couldn't believe his underage wife cheated—can't blame her there—and got pregnant. It's been the same since the dawn of humanity. Jesus was just better at marketing himself."

Nate nodded slowly and cuddled against Raz's chest, wondering how all this happened. Sure, he had thought about religion and the Bible—it came up from time to time—but he kind of shared Raziel's opinion of it. He couldn't believe something otherworldly like God or miracles happened. No, the Bible was a tool to tell people how to live, to control them—and it still worked to this day.

When Raziel winced again, Nate looked at him worried. His boyfriend's face was twisted, and he was clearly in pain and annoyed—presumably from the pain and the topic that had just come up.

"Fucking headache," Raz muttered.

"We should sleep. Maybe it'll help," Nate softly suggested, his fingertips gently caressing Raz's temple. Sometimes it helped to dull these headaches at least a little.

Raz just nodded and shuffled around a little to turn to his side, his back to the wall now. In the meantime, Nate got up to turn off the computer and light, then cuddled up against Raz and kissed his lips, full of love.

"Good night."

Raz smiled at him again, before he closed his eyes as well. Nate loved sleeping like this, having his boyfriend so close, especially now in winter. It was cozy and warm, and he always felt protected and not alone anymore. Although the worries about Raz's headaches kept circling in the back of his mind.

Nate was woken up by mumbling and a groan.

Tired and a bit disoriented, he tried figuring out what was going on and realized it was Raziel. The angel's face was distorted and sweaty, one hand balled up, and he was clearly stuck in a bad dream. Carefully, Nate shook him by his shoulder, trying to wake him up.

"It's a dream, Raz. You're okay."

It took an agonizing amount of time for Raz to finally relax and open his eyes, staring at him, confusion clouding his face. His gaze was almost blank and unfocused, as if Nate wasn't even there. He noticed the moment Raz recognized him immediately, as Raz exhaled and closed his eyes again, his fingers uncurling.

"Are you okay?" Nate asked.

Raz stared at him for a moment before he nodded slightly and pushed away a sweaty strand of hair sticking to his face. He turned on his back, the back of his hand against his forehead, and stared at the ceiling.

"I dreamed of a different place," Raz said. "It was all white and gold and blue, and there were so many other people...I think. But I felt wrong there, like an outcast. Like I didn't belong and had to get out."

The confusion and exhaustion the nightmare had left in Raz was almost palpable, his skin still damp from cold sweat. Frowning, Nate listened to the explanation. To him, it sounded a lot like Raz had dreamed of...Heaven? But why couldn't he remember it was Heaven? Maybe it was a different place after all?

"To me that sounds like Heaven?" he carefully said.

A frown formed on Raziel's face, before the angel tilted his head to Nate again. "I don't know. I don't remember."

And even though Raziel sounded so calm and like he didn't care at all, Nate could see the fear in his eyes. He was scared that he couldn't remember. But was it a bad thing to forget? Nate wasn't sure. Sometimes he wished he could forget all those years with his father, his teen years, but he couldn't. It always came back to him—it was a part of him, as were these memories Raz was dealing with.

"It's alright," Nate told him. "You don't have to remember. You have a new home."

Smiling, he leaned closer and cuddled against Raz's side, hopefully reassuring him a little and taking some of his fear and worries. He didn't want his boyfriend to suffer, didn't want him to fear that he was alone. Memories weren't too important, anyway. The present was much more relevant.

Nate just heard a hum, then an arm wrapped around him. Still, he laid awake for a long time, even after Raz had fallen asleep again. What was going on with his angel? But maybe it was a normal thing to grieve like this, his way of dealing with what had happened to him. It might even help him heal.

DECEMBER 19TH, 2023

The headaches hadn't gotten any better. On the contrary, by now, Raz needed two painkillers to make them stop, and he woke up with a headache almost every day. Nate suggested he should see a doctor but Raz had declined, assuring him it was just the stress of working so much and having so many customers.

Nate wasn't so sure about that.

There had been more nightmares as well—Raz had told him about some of them, that he'd seen strange people, some with golden eyes, some with red ones, wings and blood. It still sounded like suppressed memories to Nate, but Raz had stopped telling him any details lately. It made Nate uncertain of how to deal with Raz anymore and how to help him. He felt useless, out of his depth. To see his boyfriend suffering almost every night, basically always on pain killers, worried Nate deeply.

"What will you get Jamie?"

Raz's question pulled him from his thoughts. Nate had been staring at his fries, their lunch at work, which they were eating in the break room.

"He's talking a lot about a certain book lately," Nate said. "I contacted the author, and they agreed to sell me a signed edition, it's already on its way. I also want to get painted edges for it. Since the cover has sunflowers, maybe something with that. Jamie showed me some snippets, and they're really good. Like, unwanted divinity and a journey to find your place in the world, deciding if your freedom or your duties are more important to you. You'd probably like it, too."

Although Nate didn't read much, that book sounded interesting, and he would probably read it as well. Maybe when he was in Germany. He would have some time on the plane and when he was at his grandma's house. A lot of what he'd heard about it reminded him of Raziel, so he was even more interested.

"Sounds interesting," Raz said. "I've got no idea what sorts of gifts to give people. Especially not Jamie."

Raz sighed deeply and leaned back, crossing his legs. He looked tired, dark circles under his eyes. Last night had been fueled by another nightmare again—one Raz refused to talk about. It must've been bad, as he'd woken up with a devastating headache as well, but Nate hadn't probed. If Raz didn't want to tell him, he must have his reasons.

"He'll be happy with pretty much anything," Nate assured him. "You don't have to buy us stuff, though. It's just a stupid marketing tradition. I'm just glad when you're there with me."

That apparently wasn't the response Raz had expected or hoped for, as he frowned and got up. "I'll be downstairs. Still need to fill the fridge."

When Raz left the break room, Nate didn't get a kiss as he normally had. His eyes followed the angel, and when he heard the door close, he sighed. Once again, Raz was more silent and irritable after tossing and turning from nightmares. These moods had become the norm the last few days, and Nate couldn't even blame Raz. After nights of bad sleep, headaches, and nightmares, anyone would be irritable.

Maybe he should drag Raz to a doctor to get him checked out. Just to be safe.

CHAPTER TWENTY

Beginnings

DECEMBER 31ST, 2023

Jamie, Raziel, and Nate were all cuddled up on the couch, watching a classic black and white sketch on TV. It had become a tradition to watch this one every New Year's Eve with Jamie, and this year, Raz was also part of their tradition.

Fond memories of watching this sketch with his mom as a child left Nate with a warm feeling in his stomach. It reminded him there had been good moments in his childhood, too, no matter how much it all had gone down the drain later on. Now in his adulthood, watching the sketch had become a little drinking game, all of them taking a shot whenever the butler tripped over the tiger's head.

It wasn't surprising they were all a little tipsy once the sketch finished, but it wasn't too bad. They weren't overdoing it, were taking care of each other, and had had wonderful food before. Also, they wouldn't be drinking much more the rest of the night; they had decided on that beforehand because it was too much of a temptation for Nate.

"What time is it?" Nate asked, his fingers playing with Raz's long hair, the angel's head on his lap and legs stretched out.

"Uh, let me check." It was Jamie who stretched a little to grab his phone and check the time. "Half an hour 'til midnight."

Jamie fell back on the sofa and snagged the chips, snacking on some and offering the bag to Raz, who lazily grabbed some as well and licked his fingers after munching his snack. Nate had learned to love their little cozy moments, no matter how boring others would describe them as. Just spending time with his best friend and his boyfriend in peace was wonderful. He didn't need more people around him.

His life had changed so much within the last few months. Over the summer, he'd still been in an abusive relationship, hurting himself to cope with being hurt over and over again. Then Raz had shown up, a stranger just as battered and lost as Nate had been. With Raz's support, Nate had finally managed to escape Daniel's grasp, had started therapy, and was feeling healthier and happier every day.

The relief that came with that realization made him smile, and full of love, Nate looked down at Raz. His eyes were closed, and his expression was relaxed. Raz was the best thing that could've happened to him. After all the hurt and pain, Raziel gave him the comfort and warmth Nate had craved—and been denied—since his childhood.

He was proud of himself for taking steps to better his life. No matter how hard and painful therapy was, it had been the right decision. It would help him heal eventually. Step by step, Nate was finding himself, and there was hope inside him again—hope that had disappeared a long time ago. The year couldn't end any better than to be with Raz and Jamie around.

"You want another beer?" Jamie offered while he got up and stretched.

Pulled from his thoughts, Nate looked up from Raz's relaxed face, and his attention shifted to his best friend. Like most of the time at home, Jamie was wearing sweatpants and a hoodie with fluffy cat-paw slippers on his feet—the perfect outfit for an evening spent on the couch.

"Yeah, sure," Nate agreed, smiling. He wasn't too drunk yet, and one beer would be fine.

After Jamie went out to the kitchen, Raz's green eyes fixated on Nate. Lately, Nate had noticed the golden speckles in them slowly disappearing, but he hadn't mentioned it to Raziel yet. He wondered if the angel had noticed the change, or if maybe Nate was imagining it.

Right now, he didn't want to think about it either, especially when he felt his boyfriend's hand on his cheek, creeping higher to his nape, pulling him down into a longing kiss. Yeah, he knew how celebrating the new year would end tonight after they finished watching the fireworks. It was a good way to celebrate, one Nate could finally enjoy fully.

"Guys, come on. You can wait an hour, right?"

Jamie pouted when he came back with three beer cans, then grinned. He sat down next to Nate again and handed them both their beers. Nate grinned as well and kissed Raz again before taking a big sip from his can. Good thing Jamie had never had a problem with them being intimate, although they tried to keep their hands off each other while he was around.

Soon, they heard the first fireworks—early ones, like every year. But it meant they were very close to midnight and should get ready. This time, Nate got up first and grabbed their jackets from the hallway and put on his own. It would be too cold to stand around outside on their balcony with just a shirt or hoodie on.

After they turned off the light in the living room, they went outside onto the balcony, beers still in hand. While Jamie leaned against the railing, Nate felt an arm around his chest and Raz pressing against his back, holding him close. Happily, he smiled and turned his head a little to kiss his boyfriend before going back to watching the fireworks.

It wasn't hard to miss midnight, with all the fireworks going off simultaneously now, and despite knowing how fucked up these things were for nature and animals, Nate couldn't help but watch, mesmerized by the beauty of the vivid colors.

It was the best New Year's Eve and New Year's Day he could imagine—standing here with his best friend and his boyfriend, knowing he was actually loved and cared for by the two people he loved most. So many things had changed, and knowing he wasn't alone gave Nate confidence. There was happiness inside him, blooming gingerly, with a dire need to be cared for—but it was there.

They just watched the fireworks silently for some time, and by now, Raz had wrapped both arms around him, his chin on Nate's shoulder. It was all he needed right now, everything he had wished for today—to start the New Year with Raziel by his side.

Slowly, he turned around a little, his free hand now on Raz's neck, pulling him close and into a kiss, one that got more and more passionate, full of longing for each other and a desire to be even closer.

"Alright, I'm gonna go game now," Jamie said. "You two have fun. And don't stay outside too long; it's cold."

Jamie just pulled the empty can from his hand and grabbed Raz's before he headed inside, leaving them alone. Nate just smiled at his boyfriend, enjoying the view. Raz's face was illuminated by different colors of fireworks, red and blue and gold, his eyes sparkling in the dark. Nate couldn't believe he had such a handsome person at his side.

"Jamie's right, it's cold. Let's go to our room," Raziel suggested softly, and after Nate nodded, they both went inside as well, locking the balcony door behind them.

Their jackets landed on the couch. They could worry about tidying this up later; right now, they just wanted to get into their room. As soon as Nate closed the door, Raz's lips were on his own again.

Patience was no longer necessary, and they undressed each other frantically, touching every single speck of naked skin, exploring each other's bodies despite knowing them so well already. It was always intimate and sent shivers through Nate's whole body. To be with Raz was special, and it never felt wrong. The deep trust between them let him relax and enjoy their closeness.

Even when Nate was on his stomach, back fully exposed, he was okay. There was no lingering worry Raz could judge him or be disgusted by his scars—or, worse, hurt him. Patiently, he waited for Raz to come back over to him, since the angel had turned on the starry sky projector Jamie had gotten them for Christmas. It illuminated the room in a soft light, changing between different shades of green, blue, pink, and red. It was the perfect mixture of comfortably dark and being able to see enough of each other.

Soon enough, Raz crawled onto the bed next to Nate, soft fingers tracing his spine from his neck down to his ass, sending shivers through his body. The delicate kisses pressed into his shoulders didn't really help, and a pleased sigh signaled how content Nate was with this attention.

Raziel kissed every single one of his scars, working his way from his shoulders down to his back and finally to his butt, even kissing the scar there, before he laid down on him with almost all his weight. It was a strangely comforting thing to feel his boyfriend's body like this.

"You're so beautiful," Raz whispered in his ear, sending goose bumps over his body. His long hair tickled Nate's shoulder and neck and made the situation even more intense.

Before Nate could even think about what to say, Raz kissed his way down again and pulled him to his knees. It was such a vulnerable position, and as far as Nate remembered, this was the first time he'd actually allowed Raziel to sleep with him like this. Every other time, he'd needed to see him, to know it was really Raziel and no one else.

But today, this felt right, and Nate was ready for it. It was the beginning of a new year, a new era, and while Nate didn't believe in New Year's resolutions, he believed in trusting Raziel unconditionally. He moaned into the pillow with every thrust, every touch—it was all he wanted, all he needed.

When he was suddenly pushed over onto his back, he looked up at, Raz who grinned at him and was back between his legs in just a few seconds.

This was even better, he could see his boyfriend, touch him, hold him, pull him close to a kiss. The tips of Raz's hair tickled his chest, his hand firmly but gently grasping his thigh, and his hot breath brushed against Nate's lips.

"Raz...Raz, I love you", Nate whispered, without even thinking about it. He needed to put his feelings into words, say it out loud.

A bit uncertainly, he returned Raziel's gaze, not sure how his boyfriend would react, but finally he saw the big smile and got another kiss.

"I love you too," the angel whispered right next to his ear.

Nate moaned as they moved together, as Raz held onto him and fucked him so good. After actually confessing their feelings, after putting it into words, being so close was even more intense. Raz's low moans right in his ear, his breath against his neck, made it all so perfect.

He could do this all night, until the sun came up, and they would fall asleep exhausted, curled up into each other. The new year would be theirs, truly and fully. Nate was sure of that.

Chapter Twenty-One

Goodbye For Now

JANUARY 9TH, 2024

After yet another nightmare and more days filled with headaches, Nate decided to drag Raz to a doctor, even though his boyfriend wasn't happy about it. Instead of getting better, he got worse every day, and Nate hoped the doctor could figure out what was going on.

Many questions and tests later, the doctor was as dumbfounded as they were, so he ordered an MRI. The closest appointment available was several weeks away, which meant Raz would have to deal with his problems while Nate was away on his trip.

"You took a pill today?" Nate asked gently. He was sitting next to Raz, holding his hair back while the angel puked into the toilet.

By now, some of the headaches had become migraines, with nausea and disorientation, and Nate felt incredible helpless. He couldn't do anything but be there for Raziel and try to make him as comfortable as possible.

"Hmh, a normal one," Raz replied. "Didn't work."

Nate sighed and watched his boyfriend, who looked so tired and exhausted by all this. Once again, he wondered if it really was a good idea to leave him alone now, but the flights were already paid for, and he didn't know when he would have another opportunity to see his grandma.

Jamie had already promised to look after Raz while Nate wasn't there, and of course, they would call each other every day. Still, Nate was anxious about this trip, especially because he was visiting his home country after living abroad for half his life.

"Go get into bed," Nate said. "I'll get you a stronger pill."

Carefully, he helped Raziel up and left him to wash his face while Nate grabbed the stronger, faster working pain killer the doctor had prescribed to counter these migraines as much as possible. Nate also fetched a bottle of water and brought both back to their room, where Raz was sitting on the edge of the bed, his head propped on his hand, staring at the floor. All this sucked so much, and Raz didn't even talk about any of his nightmares anymore. He just suffered in silence, frustrated and irritated more and more every day.

"Here, take it," Nate said softly. "Then try to rest a little."

Nate handed the angel both the pill and the bottle, hoping it'd help, at least for the moment. Raz took the pill silently and swallowed it, washing it down with some water, before he laid down on the bed, his back to the door. Nate also shut the curtains, to keep the light out so Raz could relax.

"Thanks Nate," Raz murmured.

A crooked smile set on Nate's lips, and he leaned closer to kiss Raziel's temple and pull a blanket over him. Even if Raz couldn't sleep, some rest should help him until the pill did its job.

While Raziel was resting, Nate wandered into the living room and made himself comfortable next to Jamie on the couch, crossing his legs. He was glad Raz wouldn't be alone, that he would have Jamie looking out for him. Otherwise, he would have canceled his trip immediately. Leaving Raz all on his own in this condition wasn't an option.

"It's still getting worse," he lamented, feeling Jamie's questioning gaze upon him.

"Any idea what's going on with him? Is it because he's an angel, or is it some human thing?"

Nate shrugged. If he only knew, maybe he could help Raziel better. He guessed it had something to do with being an angel, especially since the nightmares—the ones Raz had told him about—often were about places and people resembling Heaven and other angels, despite Raz being unable to name or remember them.

"I don't know," Nate said. "I just hope the doctors find a way to help him."

Nate certainly didn't know how to. He was neither an angel nor a doctor; he was just a human who struggled with problems himself. At least he hadn't had a setback lately. Therapy really was helping him, as was not seeing Daniel nor his father.

He didn't want to think about any of that right now, so he changed the subject. "When's your name change date anyway?" he asked Jamie.

His friend had already gone through most of the formal procedures and was just waiting for a court date.

"Oh, early next month!" Jamie said proudly. "I can't wait to finally see my real name everywhere!" His smile grew until he was beaming. "I don't remember if I told you this, but I'm getting misgendered less and less at work now, too. Despite, y'know, not really passing."

Now Nate turned to his best friend. What was he talking about? Not passing? Jamie's voice had changed a lot already, and especially now, during winter, with all those layers of clothing, he was passing perfectly. Not that it really mattered to Nate; for him Jamie was a guy without any doubt.

Seeing the expression on Nate's face, Jamie said, "Just because a man doesn't have a full beard or isn't hairy everywhere, some people act like he's not a man. Idiots."

Nate shook his head, annoyed by such dumb people. According to that logic, no one was a "real" man. Neither he nor Raz had a beard, and they also didn't care much for any stereotypical gender stuff.

"That's ridiculous," Nate said.

"I know, I know. It's just frustrating. I'm growing hair pretty much everywhere but my face. Would prefer if it grew here." Jamie poked his cheek with one finger before he sighed and leaned back. "Not on my ass and chest." Now he was pouting a little, and Nate couldn't help but hug him.

"What genetics do to you," Nate said, understanding *that*. Even though he was cis, he had his own insecurities about his body. "But hey, your voice changed so much already. I'm sure the beard will follow."

Jamie was still pouting, and he looked at him a bit skeptically. Transitioning was obviously hard, but Nate was glad they lived in a safe enough state that his best friend could become who he was meant to be without someone trying to stop him.

He paused his video game and waved his controller at Nate. "You wanna play a little? We haven't done that in a while."

Nate would never say no to that offer and grabbed a controller while Jamie searched for a different game they could play, which ended up being one where they had to cooperate at to make any progress. Good thing they could work together...mostly.

JANUARY 14TH, 2024

The day Nate flew to Germany, Jamie said his goodbyes at home while Raziel accompanied him to the airport in Seattle. It would be hard, being apart from each other for almost two weeks; for either of them, especially with the whole world in between them.

He hadn't even left yet, and already Nate longed to be with Raz. who had become his anchor. Falling asleep with his boyfriend every single night was reassuring, and now, Nate would have to deal with almost two weeks of missing Raz.

It scared him, too, the idea of being on his own again, without the constant reminder of how much he was loved. Nate was terrified that he'd spiral back into a dark place, his head full of dark thoughts, especially since he'd be in his old hometown, where so many memories would flood back to him. He wished Raz could come with him, but it was just too expensive.

"I'll miss you so much," Nate whispered, holding onto Raz, hiding in their hug.

"I'll miss you, too. Take care of yourself and text me when you've landed." Raz loosened the hug just a little to look at him. "I got you something." His boyfriend searched in his jacket, revealing a small box.

Not expecting a gift, Nate looked up at Raz, wondering what was in the box. The thought of Raz finding a gift for him, surprising him like this, was incredibly sweet, and warm affection rushed through Nate. It was yet another reason why he loved Raz so much, always wanting to surprise him, doing these cute gestures.

Carefully, Nate took the box and opened it to find two rings inside. One was just a thin band with a cat head while the other one was thicker and had the outline of the same cat head so that they fit together like two pieces of a puzzle.

The sight of these rings, of being connected to Raz even on the other side of the world, produced a happy smile on Nate's lips. Raz really had thought about this, and it was incredibly adorable. It lifted the anxiety of being separated a little, made the moment a bit less crushing, and left Nate with a warm, fuzzy feeling.

When he looked up from the rings, Raz was grinning at him, his green eyes sparkling.

"You're so cheesy. I love it!" Nate smiled broadly and stretched just enough to kiss him gently. "I love *you*," he whispered.

There was no doubt about that; everything inside of him longed for Raz, and that his boyfriend chose cat-shaped rings fitting their nicknames made it even better.

Once their kiss ended, Raz took the smaller ring and gently pushed it on Nate's finger, then took the other one and put it on his own finger. It looked amazing on Raz's long fingers, and the small band on his own fit perfectly, too.

"So you won't forget me, kitty," Raz whispered, so softly that it melted Nate's heart.

The nickname made him chuckle as he hugged Raz again, searching for his lips and kissing him softly. Even though the rings didn't look expensive, he loved the gesture. That was much more important than the actual price.

It would always remind him that Raz was waiting for him here at home, that time apart wouldn't be for long. The dreadful feeling inside of him disappeared mostly, even as Nate had to let go to head to the security checks. They would be back together soon. It wouldn't be forever.

But still, this was goodbye. For now.

CHAPTER TWENTY-TWO

Worlds Apart

JANUARY 19TH, 2024

Being back in Germany, especially in his little hometown, was as weird as Nate had guessed it would be. It was wonderful to finally see his grandma again, although she had gotten quite frail, but he couldn't do much since it was too cold to really go outside.

When Nate wasn't talking to his grandma, he read the books he'd downloaded before his trip. Currently, he was quite invested in a sapphic Appalachian folk horror story. During the flight, he'd almost binged through an urban fantasy with more time traveling and a quite interesting character—Cade, if Nate remembered correctly. It was a relief to finally have the time and energy to read more again.

His jet lag luckily finally stopped the second day, and now, almost a week had passed already.

Nate had just woken up, ready to call his boyfriend. Their time difference was annoying, and he always had to make sure Raz wasn't at work or sleeping when he called, but right in the morning was the best time. It would be late evening at Raziel's place, so he would probably be in bed.

Of course, Nate opted for a video call; he wanted to see his boyfriend and not just hear his voice. He missed Raziel deeply, their nightly cuddles and kisses. Despite being incredibly glad to have the chance to see his grandma again, Nate would be even more glad when he could head back home.

"Hey…"

As soon as he saw Raz on the small display, he smiled and cuddled up more against the pillow while his boyfriend did the same, reciprocating his smile.

"Hey, kitty. Did you sleep well?" Raz asked softly.

How he had missed that voice throughout the previous day. To hear Raz right after he woke up was the best thing to happen to him here, and Nate could only smile.

"Yeah, but I missed you. It's a little lonely without my personal heater," Nate joked.

His grandma's house was quite cold since she still heated mostly with an old-school fireplace in the living room down-stairs. There were only two additional heaters installed in the living room and her own bedroom, but in Nate's room, on the upper floor, there was very little warmth. So Nate had to use two blankets and a radiator to keep warm.

Raziel gave a low laugh and pushed back a strand of stray hair. These little gestures were something Nate adored so much. "You'll be back soon. I can't wait to kiss you again—and do other things with you."

Now Raz smirked and made Nate grin. Yeah, he couldn't wait for that either. With Raz, his libido had rapidly increased, while Nate had barely thought about it the last few years. Every time he noticed it, he was fascinated by it. Nate had gotten so used to being around Raziel, spending every single night with him. It was really lonely to be on the other side of the world now, all by himself.

"You can do whatever you want with me when I'm back," he promised but frowned when he heard a weird noise he couldn't place. "What's that noise?" he wondered and noticed Raziel getting flustered.

"Uhm...well...y'know, I've been lonely too. So..." The angle of the video changed a little when Raziel turned his phone to show Baby sleeping and purring on his chest.

"Raz, we agreed no cats on the bed."

Nate sighed but couldn't help to smile. It was adorable, especially since Baby never slept so comfortably next to him. She really loved Raziel.

"I know, I know, but she's warm and fuzzy, and you're not here." A pout covered Raz's lips, and even if he wanted to, Nate couldn't be mad at him. "And her purring helps a little against the headaches," Raz added more quietly, like he didn't even want to mention them.

Immediately, worry surged up in Nate. Although Raz had stopped telling him about the contents of his dreams, Nate knew quite well nightmares still plagued him almost every night. He could only hope Jamie was helping Raz through them or at least giving him some pain killers.

"They're still getting worse?"

Was it even possible to get worse? Raziel already had terrible migraines; how could it get worse? It for sure didn't get better, and Nate couldn't wait for the MRI appointment.

But Raz just shrugged and didn't answer his question, which honestly was answer enough. His boyfriend truly was more the type to avoid talking about his struggles—which wasn't healthy either, as Nate well knew.

"What's the plan for today?" Raz asked, distracting from the topic of his own health—and it worked.

Right. His grandma had already required his help for some things, like tidying up her attic and getting rid of clutter because she wanted to get her affairs in order.

"She wants to go to her bank 'cause I'm supposed to inherit a bank account that's been in our family for generations," Nate explained. "She's got a whole plan for when she dies. It feels wrong to talk to her about these things—she's still *alive*—but I understand why she's doing it."

Nate huffed and turned to his side, cuddling against his pillow again. It was still a macabre thought, one he didn't even want to entertain. If he had his way, she'd live many, many more years, long enough for him to visit her again, maybe even with Raz next time.

"You said you're also going to inherit her house, right?" Raz said.

Nate nodded slightly. It was another big topic, and a lot of responsibility to handle. "Yeah, my uncle and me. He's supposed to sell it; he gets half of the money, and I get the other. She said she doesn't want me to worry about all this, not with me living abroad."

But it still felt like he was just using her for her money right now, which wasn't what Nate wanted. She'd cared for him for so many years; when his parents were working, she'd taken him home after preschool and, later, elementary school, cooking him a wonderful lunch. She'd been there for him when his mom had died. She was the one person in his family he truly loved and appreciated.

"She's not wrong," Raz told him. "It's not your fault you're so far away. Enjoy your time with her, and let her decide what she's going to do, alright? But do take her out for some good food."

Raz's last comment made him smile again and pushed the melancholic thoughts aside for now. Nate would take her out to eat, maybe even today, after their appointment at the bank. His uncle would drive them, since by now taking the bus was too much for his grandma.

"Thanks, Raz. Guess I needed to hear that." He sat up and stretched. "I better get up and help her make some breakfast. Sleep well and give Baby some chin scratches from me."

Nate kissed the tips of his middle and forefinger, pressing them against his phone camera for a moment, and saw Raz do the same. Maybe they were cheesy, but it had become their way to kiss over distance.

"I will. Love you."

"Love you, too."

Even after their call had ended, Nate stayed in bed for some more moments, staring at the ring Raziel had gifted him right before his departure. It was good to have it, to have this reminder of someone waiting for him. He felt like an alien here—not in his grandma's house, but in this town, this whole country. Especially in this corner of the country, which was openly and radically right-wing.

With a groan, Nate slowly got up and put on not just a shirt but a sweater as well. January was cold around here, not so different from his other home. But in every other way, it was like being on two different planets.

JANUARY 22ND, 2024

A few days later, Nate was exploring the town a little, just walking around long-known but almost forgotten streets, reminiscing about his childhood. He passed his uncle's house, then headed a little further, stopping right in front of his old home.

It was a big house with an even bigger property, sold when they moved to the US. Silently, he just stared down the driveway, a flush of melancholia rushing through him. How much he had loved playing in the yard with friends. Picking cherries from their old tree. Plucking carrots from their miniature field. Running around wild with their big black Newf dog and loving her like a big sister. Sitting in his room and reading books all day.

He was almost hypnotized as he fantasized about how good it could've been—if only his mother hadn't died in that car accident. All of these good recollections were overshadowed by the first time his father had burned him, turning his joyful memories to ash.

Slowly, he headed further, tearing his gaze away from his old home, burning the bridge in his mind, like he should've done long ago. He couldn't go back.

Then he stopped at a florist he spotted on the way, carefully picking out just the right flowers. Finally, he arrived at his destination. Step by step, Nate headed through the gravestones, searching for the right one—and finally found it. His mother's grave. It looked cared for, green garlands made of conifer branches covering it, the sand raked. His grandma and uncle had been caring for it, for their daughter-in-law, their sister-in-law.

Nate carefully placed the small bunch of pink and red tulips—her favorite flowers—on her grave and crouched down in front of it.

"I'm so sorry. I...I'm sorry I didn't come here earlier."

His voice was only a whisper in the cold air, his breath forming small clouds. He wasn't sure why he was even talking to her, to her grave, like he believed she could hear him.

"But I'm happy now...for the most part. I have a great best friend and a wonderful boyfriend. And I haven't seen *him* for years." He stopped, closing his eyes for a moment and covering his face in his hands. She knew who *he* was. "I wish you were there. I wish you could've stopped him. I didn't deserve any of this. I didn't do anything wrong!"

This was possibly the first time he truly allowed himself to grieve properly, for his mother, for himself, his stolen childhood and youth, all the pain he had to endure. Tears were flowing down his cheeks, wetting his palms, but Nate didn't care. Right now, he couldn't stop—didn't *want* to stop—sobbing. For once, he allowed his emotions to overwhelm him completely.

He had no idea how long he kneeled there, crying and healing, but it was good. *Right.* He had needed this moment, had craved it for so long, and maybe he could finally close this chapter of his life.

CHAPTER TWENTY-THREE

Reunion

JANUARY 25TH, 2024

Home. Finally, Nate was back in the States, although his plane had just landed, and he was still waiting to pick up his bag. But it meant he would be back to Raziel very soon, back to his own apartment, his own room.

> waiting for my bag rn

> tell me when your trains arrives
> I'll pick you up

A happy smile lifted his lips, and he couldn't wait to be back with his boyfriend, who was meeting him at the train station in Stamdon. Although they'd only been apart for a week and a half, it had felt like an eternity, and Nate longed for some kisses and cuddles.

With his bag slung over one shoulder, Nate headed to the train station close by. He felt watched, the hairs on his neck standing up, but he wasn't sure where it was coming from. No one except Raziel and Jamie knew he was coming back today, so it was probably just some stranger watching people as they passed by. But it still made Nate shiver uncomfortably.

His headphones covered his ears, and music distracted him from the other people around him, who were chattering to each other or talking on their phones. But even the distraction couldn't shake off the dreadful feeling building in his stomach. Nate headed to one of the small shops and bought a bottle of water, taking a sip while he checked the display to see which platform he had to get to. At least he had enough time that he didn't have to hurry or risk missing his train.

Once he was on the train, he was sure this dreadful feeling would disappear. The thought of seeing Raz in just an hour kept him light-hearted, overshadowing the looming darkness.

At least until something pressed into his side, and a person leaned close to him. Even before Nate turned around, he recognized the person by their smell: cold smoke mixed with a signature tangy perfume. No, this couldn't be happening. Nate's body froze, unable to react in any way, and panic rushed through him.

His headphones were pulled from his ears, and the person pressed even closer to him, whispering into his ear, "Hello, bitch. You better come with me, or I'll shoot you right here and now."

Slowly, his gaze wandered down his body to Daniel's hand holding an object obscured underneath his jacket and pressed against his side. From the shape of it, it could very well be a gun, and Nate was too afraid of what would happen if he struggled right now. He had no doubt Daniel didn't give a shit if people were watching and *would* shoot him, even in such a public place.

Daniel grinned and wrapped his second arm around Nate's shoulder, leading him outside and around the building to a darker corner, where Nate spotted his parked car. He was shivering, despite wearing a thick jacket to ward against the cold air. But this cold didn't come from outside; it radiated deep inside himself. Everything had gone so well the last months; why did Daniel have to show up *now*? Why couldn't he just give up and move on? Nate had hoped this would never happen, but the lingering aftertaste of Daniel's and Raz's argument had stayed in his mind, and he'd always sort of wondered if they'd heard the last of his terrible ex.

It was just more proof that Nate could never have good things in his life—at least not ones that lasted.

"Good boy," Daniel said menacingly. "Now, you better keep being a good boy, or I won't be so nice."

He put the gun in his waistband and grabbed some zip-ties, pulling Nate's hands behind his back and zipping them close, the plastic cutting into his flesh. Nate didn't dare say anything or move. He could only stare at his ex, eyes wide, afraid of what would happen to him.

For all he knew, Daniel would do the very same thing to him he'd always done—and after that, he would never allow Nate to live to talk about it. The realization that Nate would either die or be kept chained in some hellhole settled in slowly, but his fear didn't allow him to fight back. He was entirely frozen, his limbs numb.

A moment later, he wasn't able to speak anymore either, as there was tape covering his lips. Daniel opened the trunk of his car and pushed him inside, searching Nate's pockets until he found his phone, which he grabbed before zip-tying Nate's legs together as well.

"Very nice." Daniel's voice sent a chill down Nate's spine. "You really learned your lesson, huh?"

A wide grin from Daniel was the last thing Nate saw before the trunk lid was shut and he was engulfed in darkness. Only small holes let some light in, but he couldn't see where they were heading, despite hearing the engine and sensing every single bump of the road.

Nausea rose up in him, and Nate tried to pull against the zip-ties, but they only cut into his flesh more. He wasn't even able to rip off the tape on his mouth. He couldn't scream, couldn't move. There was no way to escape his abductor.

AFTER WHAT FELT LIKE an eternity, the car finally came to a stop, and the engine was turned off. The thump of the door being forcefully shut and the sound of voices mixed, but Nate didn't recognize who Daniel was talking to or what was being said. So he wasn't working alone? Someone was in on this with Daniel? It made sense; Daniel was never the type to plan anything—he lived in the moment and didn't care for consequences. But who else would have a reason to abduct Nate? *That's* what didn't add up, and it only heightened his fear of what would happen next.

When the trunk was opened, Nate had to squint because the light was suddenly too bright.

"You actually managed to get him. I'm impressed." The stranger's voice was dark and he sounded more like he was talking to a subordinate than a partner. Was Daniel doing this *for* someone?

Slowly, Nate's eyes got used to the light again, but before he could look around, he was lifted out of the trunk and slung over Daniel's shoulder.

"Damn, you've gotten fat," Daniel huffed in complaint as he carried him inside...the old factory?

Nate recognized this place. He'd found Raziel here, had often come here even before that when he needed some alone time—time away from Daniel. That ripped another hole in Nate's heart, the idea of his former safe space being desecrated and used for whatever nefarious plans these two had.

Steps echoed off the bare stone floor in front of them, but Nate couldn't see the person leading the way. Whoever this was, he had more of a plan than Daniel, and it scared Nate. If it had been only Daniel, he would've known what to expect—not *nice* things, obviously, but at least things he'd gotten used to.

"Put him on the chair and zip up his legs first," the stranger instructed.

When Nate was placed on a wooden chair and the ties around his ankles cut, he tried running. He didn't know what they wanted to do with him, but he also didn't want to find out. He barely managed to stand up, his legs numb from fear and from being restricted, but adrenaline rushed through him, urging him to flee before it was too late. Hands on his shoulders forced him to sit back down and held him in place firmly and with so much strength that it felt more like a machine than a human. Daniel crouched in front of him and zipped his legs to the chair.

"Get rid of his jacket and sweater," the stranger said. "It'll make for some more urgency."

The stranger let go of him and walked around the chair, and finally Nate could see more details. It was a tall man wearing a gray suit that was perfectly tailored to his muscular body and matching gray shoes. Even his locs were the same gray, almost blending into the fabric, making his dark skin stand out even more. But what stood out most were his golden eyes. An angel? But *why*? What was going on? Why had an angel had him kidnapped? As much as he wanted to deny it, it was undeniably an angel standing in front of him, watching him with an amused smirk.

Dumbfounded, Nate didn't even try fighting Daniel, who cut the zip-ties around his wrists and took off his jacket. The sharp jackknife Daniel drew from his pants caught Nate's attention. Desperate to at least speak, Nate's hand reached for the tape covering his lips, but Daniel pressed the tip of the knife against his chest.

"Don't you dare, bitch. Be a good boy, hm?"

Nate's hands were trembling as he let them slowly fall back at his sides. He wanted to live, wanted to see Raz again, and if it meant enduring whatever these two had planned for him, so be it. Daniel grinned, satisfied, and the blade cut into the seam of his sweater and shirt.

Tears welled up in Nate's eyes as he realized his clothes were being cut open—the shirt a gift from Raz, with a cute cartoon kitty printed on it—then pulled from his body and carelessly thrown aside. As soon as the icy air hit Nate's now bare chest, goose bumps covered him, and the cold crept into his body.

With his hands zipped to the chair, Nate was left unable to move once again, and resignation set in. Either they'd kill him right here, or he would freeze to death—if they didn't plan to take him somewhere else first.

The angel nodded contentedly and grabbed a Polaroid camera, taking a picture of Nate. Once it was fully developed, the angel strode closer to him and turned the picture to him, so he could look at himself. How embarrassing he looked, zipped tight to the chair, mouth covered with tape, fear and tears in his eyes, a small trail of blood pouring from his chest where Daniel's knife had pressed into his skin.

The angel smiled broadly at him. "Perfect. You make wonderful bait, dear human." Then he took a pen from his pocket and scribbled a message on the edge of the picture. "Love, do you want to deliver this? It's an invitation for our lovely outcast."

Nate hadn't realized there was yet another person around, a woman wearing black hotpants and a crop top, only a plush pink jacket shielding her from the cold. She had long, curled pink hair, and she smiled excitedly when the angel showed her the picture. "Oh, lovely! Can I play with him when I'm back?" she wondered, strolling closer to Nate and leaning down to him.

Now Nate could see her eyes—blood red, like the shirt Raziel loved to wear. Who was she? What did they want from him?

Her attitude unsettled Nate even more, and he wished he would've fought Daniel at the train station. Either he would've died, or people would've helped him. It was too late for regrets, but he couldn't help cursing himself for his stupidity.

The angel shrugged. "Sure, I don't have any use for him anymore."

Apparently this made the woman very happy, since she smiled brightly and almost danced back to the angel. After a passionate kiss, she took the picture and headed outside.

Nate's brain was slowly catching up with what was going on, and now his heart thundered in his chest. They'd said that he was being used as some kind of bait, but he only now understood that he was bait for *Raziel*. "Outcast." It should've rung a bell the moment he heard it, but Nate had been too scared and confused for it to register.

He didn't care anymore what happened to him; he was more worried about Raz. If his boyfriend followed this bait, what would they do to *him*? It was enough reason for Nate to struggle against his restraints and try to scream through the tape, but the plastic only cut deeper into his flesh, and a harsh slap on the face from Daniel made him wince.

"Shut the fuck up," Daniel grumbled and turned to the stranger.

With his cheek pounding from the slap, Nate looked up at Daniel, noticing how annoyed he looked. That was never a good sign, although this time, the glare wasn't meant for Nate but the angel.

"You promised me he was mine after you've lured your outcast in," Daniel reminded the angel in a pissed tone.

Nate wasn't sure what was worse—being the strange woman's play toy or being in Daniel's hand again. He at least knew what Daniel might do to him, though that didn't comfort him much. Both ideas made him shiver and stirred more fear in him, but he didn't dare fight again. There was no use in it; the restraints were too tight, his legs too numb. He'd never escape Daniel *and* the angel.

"Sure, do whatever you want. I don't care." The angel just shrugged and made himself comfortable on another chair.

Daniel grinned and crept toward Nate. He pulled a chair close, sat down next to him, and got his pack of cigarettes from his pocket. No, *anything but that*. Nate choked on his own tongue as he fought against the panic, while Daniel lit a cigarette and took a deep drag, then blew the smoke into Nate's face.

The sound of the lighter and the smell of the smoke triggered Nate's panic immediately. He thought he could control his panic, that he would never experience this torture again, but Daniel was reminding him that he certainly wasn't free—that he would *never* be free. His muscles were sore, tense, and his breathing got faster while he stared at Daniel in fear, expecting pain any moment now.

These reactions were so engraved into his whole being that he couldn't stop them, didn't know how to work against them, and every single cloud of smoke made it worse. The sudden burning pain right in the crook of his neck made him scream against the tape, tears inevitably rolling down his cheeks.

But Daniel only laughed and grabbed his chin, forcing him to look up. "That's how it's gonna be. You're my toy, and you never should've thought differently."

Nate would never escape this cycle. Daniel always found him *again and again*, pushing him down and using him, marking him once more. Even if Nate was found here, he wasn't sure he could recover from this. He didn't want Raziel to come here, to get himself into danger again, just because of him. Nor did he want Raz to see the broken shards of himself, strewn across the room, as Daniel kept torturing him relentlessly.

It was better if Raz stayed away and left him to his fate.

Even if Raz had saved him before, there was nothing left to save this time.

Chapter Twenty-Four

Traitor

Nate couldn't say how long they were just sitting around. It had gotten dark some time ago, and only some makeshift lamps were illuminating the broken-down walls of the old factory. Nate was sporting several new burn marks on his neck and shoulders, and his shivering had stopped some time ago. Exhaustion had set in, and his head just hung down.

When the woman returned, Nate barely registered her kissing the angel or what the two of them were talking about with Daniel. He didn't really care anymore. Logically, he knew it was hypothermia setting in, but what could he do? He couldn't get his jacket or sweater back. At least the burns didn't really hurt anymore. Although he couldn't feel his hands and feet either.

"Aw, come on," Daniel whined. "You got such a pretty girl. Let me have a taste!"

Slowly, Nate looked up, his gaze unfocused. The woman sitting on the angel's lap was looking Daniel up and down now. She frowned at his sweatpants and generally leisurely appearance before turning toward her partner.

"Can I play with him?" she wondered in a high-pitched voice that made Nate's ears hurt.

"Do whatever you want," the angel said. "I have no use for him anymore."

For a moment, Nate wondered what that meant and just watched, although it was exhausting to keep his head upright. The woman got up and came closer to Daniel, smiling sweetly at him. And judging by Daniel's grin, that's *exactly* what he wanted.

"You want to play with me?" she wondered, taking his hands and placing them right on her chest.

Nate wondered why she wasn't freezing in her crop top and hot pants, but then again, she probably wasn't human either, considering her unusual eyes.

"Hell yeah, that's what I'm talking about," Daniel murmured and squeezed her boobs, trying to kiss her.

She put a hand on his chest. "Hell, now that you mention it…"

A bright smile spread across her bloodred lips, and she took a step back before her right arm moved faster than Nate could process. Confused, he blinked, trying to figure out what was happening.

A weird, wet sound came from Daniel, and Nate finally understood, though he wished he didn't. Panic rose in him again and he knew that whatever those two had planned for him, it would be *much* worse than anything Daniel had ever done.

The woman's hand was stuck deep inside Daniel's chest, and when she pulled it out again, leaving a big gaping wound, she had an organ in her hand, blood dripping onto the floor. Daniel fell to the floor, his eyes dulling, his body twitching a little before it fell still. No matter what Daniel had done to him, Nate would never have wished that on him.

The angel sighed, though he made no move to get up. "You're always so messy," he complained.

Despite the initial shock of it all, relief that Daniel could no longer hurt him flooded through Nate. But then the panic rose up again. What would happen to him now? Would he suffer the same fate? No matter how bad Daniel had been—what he had done—this couple wouldn't hesitate to rip out Nate's heart.

The woman, who Nate guessed had to be a demon, squeezed the heart in her hand several times, blood squirting from it, and giggled before she just threw it next to Daniel's head, blood still pouring from the hole in his chest.

The sight made Nate nauseous, and he kept his flickering attention on his captors. Nate desperately hoped Raz wouldn't come here. No matter what they had planned for him, it wouldn't be good, and Nate couldn't stand the thought of being responsible for Raz getting hurt.

"He annoyed me! I can't help it." The high-pitched voice rang in his ears, followed by a dramatic sigh, and Nate watched as the demon sat on the angel's lap again. She kissed him and placed her bloody hand on his shoulder, leaving red handprints.

"You're getting me all dirty," the angel whispered but just grinned and pulled her closer, into a more intense kiss.

Nate was confused. This guy was supposed to be an angel, wasn't he? So why did he seem to actually *like* this? Hell, why was he with a demon in the first place. Who was this angel and why was he...*like this?* Something wasn't adding up here. Angels weren't supposed to be bloodthirsty; they were supposed to be protective of humans...right?

But Nate's brain was too slow to put all the pieces together and too exhausted and cold to really process what was happening.

Then a loud voice rang out through the building, demanding, "Let Nate go or I'll kill you both!"

Raziel.

A mix of relief and fear surged up in Nate. Raz should've stayed away, kept himself safe. Nate wasn't worth saving, not for the price of possibly dying.

He turned his head a little to see his boyfriend and found him standing in the opening that used to be a door, holding a handgun aimed at these two. Where had he gotten a gun? Nate didn't know, and he didn't really care, either. Instead, he tried pulling on his ties, unsure if he was actually moving his hands at all. He couldn't really feel his limbs anymore.

"Ah, Raziel, there you are." The angel pushed his demon girl-friend from his lap and stood up, smiling broadly at Raziel. "What took you so long?"

"Do I know you?" Raz asked. "Why did you kidnap Nathaniel?"

Raz's brows were furrowed in a mix of anger, confusion, and fear, but his hands looked steady—at least from where Nate was sitting. His sight was blurry, and he couldn't quite tell. What confused him was that Raziel didn't recognize this angel. Did he not know who it was? Or had he forgotten?

The stranger laughed, then gave a cocky smile. "So, your brain's become a mush, huh? What a sad, pathetic little human you've become. We're brothers, you and I. You fell, remember? I caused your fall, but you weren't sent to Purgatory like I wanted. We can change that, now. You can't kill me with your little human weapon."

One step after another, the angel got closer to Raziel, who looked from him to the girl to Nate, until his gaze finally stopped on the other angel again. A name…Raziel had mentioned the name of the angel who caused his fall, but Nate couldn't remember it.

"I might not be able to kill you," Raz said, "But her?"

Bang.

It took Nate a moment to understand Raziel had fired a shot, not aiming at the other angel anymore but the demon woman, shooting her straight in the head. She looked confused, stretching a hand out to the gray-clad angel, before she just slumped to the ground, her pink hair surrounding her like a field of fallen cherry blossoms.

The loud noise made Nate twitch in surprise, and his eyes were wide open, staring at the second corpse. Raz had just killed a demon, and Nate wasn't so sure it was a good idea. He didn't understand much about angels and demons, but the stranger had cared about the woman in some way. He wouldn't be happy about this, and Raz was in no state to actually fight him.

Fear of what would happen fell over Nate, and he wished he could do more than just sit there, tied to a chair, his limbs numb and unresponsive. He wanted to protect Raz, wanted to run far away from the murderous angel—especially when he glared at Raziel, hatred in his golden eyes.

"You're dead!" the stranger growled.

Several more shots hit the angel, leaving bloody red marks on his suit, but he didn't stop stalking over to Raziel until he was close enough to grip him by the throat. This couldn't be happening. Nate screamed against the tape over his mouth, pulled at the ties, but there was no way to get free, to help Raziel.

Panic pushed Nate to struggle against the ties, fueled by Raz's similarly panicked expression, the gun clattering from the angel's hands to the ground.

"You were supposed to go to Purgatory for your—for *my*—crimes!" the angel hollered. "But they were lenient on you. Now I'll put you there myself!"

A gurgle came from Raziel as he tried to pry the angel's fingers from his neck, and a muffled scream could be heard before Raziel was sent flying through the room. Something cracked as Raz landed on his side and rolled onto his back, but before he could get up again, the strange angel was on top of him.

Nate spotted the panic on Raz's face, the same that tore him apart inside, as the angel tried to shield himself from the sharp nails clawing at his clothes, tearing them off and revealing more and more skin. Tears spilled over Nate's cheeks; he could only watch and scream as Raz desperately tried to fight back but to no avail.

None of this should've happened. Why had Raz come here? Why did everything In Nate's life turn to shit sooner or later?

The angel tore Raziel open, his pained screams echoing in Nate's ears as the blood-thirsty angel's hand sunk deep into Raz's stomach, blood pouring onto the ground. A rapidly growing puddle of red formed underneath Raziel.

The agonizing screams made Nate's blood curdle, and once again he tried escaping his own ties. He wanted to throw himself between the feral angel and his boyfriend, to protect Raz with his own life, but Nate only managed to fall over onto his side, still strapped to the chair. He was so useless in this confrontation, as he had been useless and weak against Daniel. There was nothing Nate could do but be used and played with, and the sudden realization only fueled his despair. He couldn't lose Raziel now—he was lost without his guardian angel.

Raziel's movements got slower, more and more blood leaving his body. The angel's gray suit was now drenched in blood, a manic expression clouding his face.

"That's enough!" someone shouted.

Nate couldn't see the person the voice belonged to, and he didn't really care either. His gaze was still fixed on the angel and Raziel, whose movements and resistance dulled with every heartbeat.

"Take him," that same unfamiliar voice ordered.

Two people Nate had never seen before hurried over to the angel, grabbing him and pulling him away, despite his efforts to break free and jump back onto Raziel. Raz was barely moving anymore, and he stared aimlessly at the ceiling. A click sounded, and chains bound the angel now, his hands tied behind his back, anger twisting his face.

For a moment, Nate glanced at the other two corpses—the demon lady, who laid motionlessly staring at the ceiling, and Daniel, with his heart next to him. So much blood and pain—for what?

"Maalik," that unfamiliar voice said, "you are hereby detained for collaborating with and bedding a demon, attacking one of your own, and dragging humans into your mess. Take him away."

Maalik, right; that was the name Nate had been searching for. It didn't matter really. What mattered was Raziel, who was still bleeding, a low moan escaping him. Even the sound of big wings taking flight didn't break Nate's concentration on his dying boyfriend.

The person taking command walked around Nate, not sparing him a glance, and kneeled down next to Raziel, where she placed her hand on his forehead. "Stay still. You're not dead yet."

It was Kundaliel. Nate dimly remembered her. At her touch, Raz's breathing relaxed, and his face didn't look as contorted in pain as before. What was she doing? Whatever it was, it eased Nate's worries—Raziel would survive, and that was the only important thing.

Whatever was to come now, they would get through it. Even if Nate was broken beyond repair, it didn't matter. Only Raz's safety was important.

Again, Nate pulled on his ties, wanting to run to his boyfriend, even if he had to take the chair with him. He didn't care, he just wanted to be with Raz, make sure he was okay. The golden eyes turned to him, and now Nate noticed that Raz's wounds were already healing, the tears Maalik had left closing up.

"His wounds will heal," Kundaliel said. "But we have a lot to discuss. I will take you both to Heaven."

Even if he was able to protest, Nate was sure she wouldn't listen to him. Heaven? But how? A strange feeling encompassed him, and warmth surrounded him. It was bright, too bright for his eyes, and Nate squeezed them shut.

But he didn't open them again. Instead, he drifted into the darkness, surrounding him, his senses useless, and his thoughts mushy. What was happening to him?

CHAPTER TWENTY-FIVE

Die For You

RAZIEL

When Raziel opened his eyes, he was in a room furnished with a big bed and a table laden with bowls of fresh fruits and carafes of different liquids, some steaming, some not. His fingers wandered to his stomach, but there was no wound there, only smooth skin. He must've been healed fully, spared from death by Maalik's hand.

Raz pushed himself up from the bed and spotted Nate lying next to him, the ties and tape gone. Slowly, Raz stretched out a hand to touch his cheek, but it was ice-cold. Cold as...a corpse. Panic built in his chest when Raz pressed his fingers against Nate's neck, searching for a pulse. He found none. Neither could he hear a heartbeat, not even when he pressed his ear against Nate's chest.

"He is not gone—yet." Kundaliel stood next to a door and watched him, only now coming closer, her golden eyes on Raziel. "He's in the place in-between."

"Bring him back then!" he demanded, unable to hide the panic and worry in his voice. He wouldn't let Nate die here. Not like this. Not because Maalik wanted *him* and had used Nate to draw him in.

Kundaliel just tilted her head and watched him curiously, no empathy to be seen at all. Angels had no capacity for it, neither did they care for a single human life. No, they thought of humans as toys or cute animals; they were to be protected as a race, but it didn't matter if one or two died here and here. It was a philosophy Raziel no longer shared.

"I won't," Kundaliel said. "You, on the other hand—you could, after Maalik's trial. If he's found guilty, your grace will be returned, and you'll come back home to Heaven as an angel. That's what you wanted all along, isn't it? You can save this human—but it will cost your own humanity."

Disbelievingly, Raz's eyes darted to Kundaliel. He didn't want to return to Heaven, become a mindless puppet and warrior again. He wanted to live his human life, to enjoy all the little joys and sorrows with Nate. But if Nate was no longer alive, none of that mattered.

"Please, Kundaliel. Please save him. I can't go back to Heaven."

He was begging now. An Archangel begging a lesser angel—how pathetic of him. Raziel didn't care. He wanted Nate to survive, wanted to save him and their love, their life together.

She shook her head. "No. You know the price. It's on you to decide what's more important to you."

A pained sob escaped his throat before Raz pressed a hand against his lips, silencing himself. He wouldn't give Kundaliel the satisfaction of seeing him cry. He'd already begged, and it had gotten him nowhere.

There was only one way.

Gently, he pulled the blanket over Nate's cold, bruised body and placed a kiss on his pale forehead. Then he got up and turned to Kundaliel, his face a cold mask.

"I will save his life," he vowed, "even if I have to die for it."

"Good. Get dressed. The trial is about to begin."

Raziel grabbed the garments he'd been provided—a white suit with golden embroidery. His old clothes, fitting for an Archangel. One last long gaze at Nate's lifeless silhouette reminded him why he'd agreed to these conditions, why he was ready to give up everything he had fought for these last months. Raz had learned to love, and he would do anything for the man he cherished.

ONCE RAZIEL WAS READY, he followed Kundaliel through some hallways with the same sort of bland décor you find in big office buildings: white carpet and walls, barren except for some landscape paintings. Raziel knew that underneath all that Heaven still looked the same; this was just how it appeared to human eyes—eyes Raz still possessed.

Their destination looked a lot like a big office as well, tables and chairs forming a half-circle around Maalik, who was standing in the middle, chained, gagged, and stripped naked.

"Sit. We are about to begin."

Kundaliel pointed to a chair close to the middle, where Raz sat down. He wasn't nervous; he knew Maalik was guilty. But he also remembered his own trial, the painful memories flooding back to him: standing in the middle, stripped naked, without any way to defend himself, judgment being passed on him, leading to his unjust fall. He still sensed all these judging golden eyes upon him—some with compassion, others with disgust, and even others with pure hatred. By now, Raziel was glad about his fall, about losing the home he'd known for eons, since the beginning of his existence.

He dreaded coming back home. The memories suffocated him, too much for his human brain to comprehend them all. His head started hurting again, but Raziel didn't even care. He would rather deal with this pain for the rest of his human life, by Nate's side, than be part of Heaven again.

"We hereby commence the trial of the angel, Maalik," Kundaliel said. "We call Raziel, fallen Archangel and Keeper of Secrets, to the stand. Get up."

To hear his full title, to remember who he used to be, pained Raziel even more. Still, he had been framed for crimes, had fallen. Titles didn't do shit.

Kundaliel's golden eyes were on him as Raziel got up from his chair, drawing the attention of all the other pairs of golden eyes in the room. They looked curious, some confused, but what did it matter? Raz had no intention of giving a fuck—he only wanted to save Nate. To prove his innocence had become secondary to him.

"I need you to remember right now," Kundaliel said. "I know remembering hurts, but you have to push through that now. Tell us everything that happened between you and Maalik."

Raziel nodded slightly and closed his eyes for a moment—not just to remember better, but to escape the gazes of too many pairs of eyes as well. He didn't want to see his brothers and sisters staring at him, passing judgment.

Slowly but steadily, Raziel laid out everything. Years ago, he had caught Maalik fooling around with demons, bedding them and collaborating with them on several schemes. No one had believed him when he reported these crimes. On their half-century trip to

Earth, Maalik had rounded up some humans to form some kind of fight club, delighting in their despair and pain, deleting the memories of the survivors after the fights, and once again fooled around with a demon.

Again, Raziel had reported it, but this time Maalik had managed to frame him, causing the trial to be cut short, without providing any evidence, resulting in Raziel's fall. He still didn't know how Maalik had managed to frame him so easily, without the authority an Archangel possessed. In hindsight, Raz realized there might be more scheming in Heaven than he'd anticipated.

The more Raz remembered, the more it hurt, the memories rushing into his mind, over-straining its capabilities. Remembering all this was agonizing, but finally Raz was allowed to sit down again, and he took a deep breath before gritting his teeth. The whispering around him grew—people chattering about if he was lying or not—but Maalik's still bloodied body should surely be evidence enough that he was the culprit, not Raz.

"We have heard all witness reports," Kundaliel announced. "The demon Maalik had been bedding is dead, but it doesn't erase his crimes. All who vote for Purgatory, lift your hand."

One hand after the next rose up, among them Raziel's, despite him not looking up and holding his head in his other hand in a futile attempt to banish the pulsing headache.

"So, it's decided. Maalik, you will be banished to Purgatory, your wings burned, and your grace taken." Kundaliel got up and stopped in front of Raz. "Close your eyes, or they'll get burned out."

Raz only had a moment to oblige before he saw a blazing light, even through his closed eyes. He knew what was happening;

Maalik's grace was forcefully being ripped out of him, his angelic powers bottled up to be stored away.

"It is done. Your grace is gone, and you'll be taken to the portal now."

Good thing Maalik was gagged, or they would hear his curses even louder. Slowly, Raziel opened his eyes again and saw several angels dragging Maalik out of the room, while Kundaliel held a small bottle in her hand, a glowing, swirling liquid inside of it. She handed it to Mitzrael, a handsome angel with shoulder-length, wavy dark hair, who hurried out of the room with the bottle in hand.

For a moment, Raz wondered why Kundaliel led all these trials, why she had so much power. She wasn't even an Archangel, one of the oldest angels, and yet everyone listened to her. The crushing headache didn't allow for him to dwell on the thought, and his attention shifted to Kundaliel.

"Now on to you," she said. "Your grace will be returned, and you'll join our ranks again. You may save your human toy, but you will never see him again after today."

Raziel had known these conditions when he'd agreed to come back to Heaven. He had no other choice if he wanted to save Nate, but even through the pain in his head, it hurt. It hurt so much to imagine a future without Nate by his side, just never-ending loneliness awaiting him. None of his siblings would be able to fill this void or give him the same love Nate had shown him.

Kundaliel urged him to get up and follow her to a room filled with many bottles like he had just seen, stored neatly next to each other on shelves covering the walls. So many angels had been stripped of their grace, but Raz knew now that it was a blessing to be free of the chains Heaven put around their necks.

Kundaliel searched around before she took a bottle and handed it to Raziel. Silently, he stared at the liquid swirling inside, light blue mixed with gold, so tempting and yet invoking fear and nausea inside him.

"What are you waiting for?" she asked. "Take it. It's yours."

His eyes darted to Kundaliel just for a moment before they landed back on the small bottle. It was calling to him, urging him to take it back. With a silent sigh, Raz pushed the cork open and let his grace flow back into his body, filling every fiber with raw, angelic power.

It hurt as much as having his grace taken, more and more memories rushing back into his mind—memories of killing hundreds and hundreds of humans, of fulfilling Heaven's mission, of Nate finding him, caring for him, always being there when he didn't know who he was anymore.

The bottle in his hand burst into hundreds of shards, and with a desperate scream, four golden wings unfolded from his back, filling most of the small room. Raz's forehead burned like it was being torn open from the inside. When he looked up, he really *saw* Kundaliel, her aura wavering around her, and the room distorted into Heaven—the *real* Heaven that could only be seen by angelic eyes—blazing white and golden.

"You have two hours to save your human and say your goodbyes," Kundaliel said. "Once he's back home, he won't remember you ever existed. Neither will any other human you've been in contact with."

Without a word, Raziel turned around, his wings neatly tucked behind his back, to head back to Nate. He would save him, even though it would cost him his humanity, even though he would be falling into darkness—even though endless loneliness was all that awaited him.

When he sat down next to Nate, Raz placed his hand on his forehead, a golden glow emanating from it, and searched for his soul to guide it back home. Slowly, warmth was returning to Nate's body, and he was breathing again.

I could lie awake all my life just to watch you breathe, he thought, his hand still on Nate's forehead. It felt good just to be close to Nate. He had to enjoy these last moments with Nate.

CHAPTER TWENTY-SIX

The Price To Pay

JANUARY 25TH, 2024

Slowly, the darkness around Nate's senses subsided, and he felt a warmth like a golden glow and heard someone calling his name. Without thinking about it, he followed the familiar glow and finally emerged from the darkness. He could breathe again, and very slowly, he opened his eyes.

Confusion still clouded his mind when he saw a white ceiling, golden stucco where it met the walls, and when he turned his head, Nate saw a person sitting next to him. It took him a long moment to recognize who it was. He looked so different.

"Raziel..." he finally whispered, forcing his hand to stretch and touch his partner, to make sure he really was here, was really real. "Am I dead?" Nate wondered.

Slowly, his sight adjusted and he recognized more differences in the man—the angel—he loved. Raz's skin wasn't a warm cream color anymore but a deep, dark blue, almost black like a night sky, and there were small golden dots across the back of his hand. It almost looked like the canvas of the universe.

He was wearing a weird, white suit with golden embroidery, perfectly fitted to his body. His piercings were gone, but four big golden wings poked out from behind his back and—an audible gasp escaped Nate when he saw Raziel's eyes. The beautiful dark green was gone, and instead, a glowing gold had replaced it, filling Raz's eyes completely. Right over the knit of the angel's perfectly framed brows, a third eye had opened, as golden as the other two.

"What...happened?"

He could spot the sad smile on Raziel's full lips, so familiar to him but still so different now, tinted a dark blue as well. Everything about Raziel was different, even more perfect than he had been before. The golden freckles across his skin emanated a faint golden glow.

"You're not dead," Raz explained. "You almost died, but I saved you. My grace was returned to me, and I'm back home."

Even though that sounded like it was a good thing, Nate still noticed the deep sadness underneath the words. Why was Raz sad? Hadn't he wanted to get back home? Back to Heaven? No, Raz had said once he didn't want to go back to Heaven, that he enjoyed the mundane human life he had with Nate.

"You're beautiful," Nate breathed. "Your eyes..."

Nate had never seen such eyes. Even Kundaliel had different eyes, just her irises golden, not the sclera as well.

"I'm an Archangel," was Raziel's only explanation for that.

Slowly, Nate sat up a little more so he could see Raz better. He touched his face, then, carefully his hand wandered further, inspecting the wings as well. So soft. He hadn't expected that from golden feathers. Raziel spread his wings a little to give him more space to explore, and Nate couldn't resist touching them all over, his fingertips brushing against them.

Meanwhile, Raz's fingers traced his shoulder, leaving a tingling sensation, and when he ended up at his wrist, Nate could see a faint golden glow. The marks from where he had been tied up disappeared, and instead, a small tattoo of a semicolon appeared next to his scar.

This was amazing. He didn't know angels were so powerful—or so beautiful—in their whole true form. Did all angels look like this once they shrugged off human disguises?

"Nathaniel..." Raz sighed. "We have to talk."

At the sound of his full name, Nate sat up straighter and looked at Raziel, his eyes wandering to the golden eye on Raz's forehead for a moment. Of course they had to talk. Raz was an angel again, and surely he couldn't just walk around like this on Earth. They had to figure out a way to disguise him. Right?

As if Raziel had heard his thoughts, he gently shook his head. "Nate... I won't be returning to Earth. Having my grace back means I'll join the ranks of Heaven again. I saved you, so you can live your life to the fullest, but I can't be a part of it anymore. This is goodbye."

Wait. Maybe he was still dreaming. Raziel wasn't coming back with him? He was just going to abandon him? Silently, Nate stared at the angel and didn't quite know what to say. A deep sorrow settled in his guts as Nate realized this was real. Raz was going to leave him after everything they've been through. Once again, he'd be entirely on his own. This was exactly what he'd been so afraid of, and now his worst nightmare was coming true. Tears formed in his eyes, spilling over.

"You should've let me die then," Nate seethed. "Without you, there's nothing to live for."

Raz sighed softly and wrapped his arms around Nate, pulling him close. The warmth didn't help to calm him down this time, not when it might be the last time he could experience one of Raz's hugs.

"Don't say that, Nate," Raz pleaded. "You'll find love again. You won't know I was in your life. You won't even miss me."

What was Raziel talking about? All of this was wrong, so incredibly wrong. His hands grabbed onto Raz's suit. It looked so incredibly ridiculous and absolutely not like Raz at all. He didn't want to let go; he only wanted to stay with Raziel. Tears flowed over his cheeks, soaking Raz's suit, and his heart ached.

"But I don't want to forget you!" Nate cried.

A choked sob escaped him, and Raz squeezed him even tighter in his embrace. It was so protective and loving, and Nate had become used to it, had taken it for granted. How could he live without Raziel, without his guardian angel by his side?

He let go, just a little, so he could see Raziel better. He thought it'd be hard to figure out emotions in these golden eyes, but it wasn't. Raziel's tears—not clear like his own, but a thick, golden liquid—poured down his cheeks and bridge of his nose.

"Promise me you won't do anything stupid," Raz whispered, his voice wavering. His warm hand was on Nate's face, a thumb brushing away the tears. "I'll always keep watch over you." Raz brushed his thumb over the fresh tattoo, the mark on his wrist. "This is *my* promise."

"I...I'll try. I can't promise."

He sometimes did dumb things without even intending to do so. Raziel had rescued him, more than once. He wasn't sure how he could survive on his own. But Raziel just nodded and pulled him close again, into a desperate kiss.

Nate wasn't sure how long they sat there, just holding each other, crying and kissing.

"It's time."

The voice from the door made him wince, and he pressed closer to Raziel again, holding onto him, afraid of what was to come. Maybe if he just held onto Raz strong enough, he could escape this scheme. But logically, Nate knew angels were much stronger than him. and it wouldn't make any difference.

"Please...please don't do this. *Please* let me remember him," Nate begged, but Kundaliel's golden eyes were still as stern as before, no empathy to be seen.

"Remember, Raziel," she said, "it's easy to let one human disappear. Don't ever forget that."

What was that supposed to mean? Confused, Nate looked up at Raz, who had his eyes closed now, a pained expression on his face.

"If you ever dare to hurt Nathaniel, I will wreak havoc on Heaven," Raziel whispered, his golden eyes now on the other angel, and even though it was hard to distinguish, Nate could recognize blazing hatred.

Once Raz turned his attention to Nate, his expression shifted immediately to a much softer and more loving one, although it was clouded over by a profound sadness.

"I am so sorry, Nate. I love you, and I will forever love you," Raz whispered and kissed him again, desperately.

When Nate felt the angel's warm hand on his forehead, everything went black again.

NATE WOKE UP ON his bed with what felt like the worst hangover he'd ever had. Groaning, he turned on his side and kept still, just staring on the wall. His mind felt mushy, like things were missing, but he couldn't exactly place where this feeling was coming from.

With an annoyed grumble, he got up slowly and headed to the kitchen, where Jamie was already preparing breakfast.

"Good morning, sleepyhead. Still got jetlag?"

Jetlag? Oh, right, he'd just come back from visiting his grandma yesterday. Might explain why he was so unbelievably exhausted. Nate just plopped down on a chair, resting his chin on his hand.

"Maybe. I'm just feeling weird. Like...I'm missing something?"

It was hard to describe. It just felt like something dear to him was gone, but he couldn't quite grasp what it was or where this feeling came from. He just felt empty. Alone. Even though his best friend was in the same room with him.

"We could go to a party this weekend," Jamie said. "You might find someone to flirt with there. You need some better company than Daniel was. Good thing that asshole's gone."

Daniel? Nate frowned and tried to remember what the hell had happened to his ex. He could recall seeing him several months ago, being his usual fucked up self.

"What happened to him? Sorry, my brain's really mushy today."

An apologetic smile hit Jamie, and when his best friend turned around to him, he had a skeptic frown on his face, which soon turned sympathetic.

"It's fine," Jamie assured him. "No wonder you forgot about him after everything. He was found dead a few weeks ago after he wrecked his car. The police suspect he was on his way to kidnap you. There was a gun and zip ties in his car."

Right, now he remembered. The police had questioned him since his name had been all over Daniel's phone and notes. What a fucked-up guy he was, obsessed to the end. Nate really was glad he was gone. Although Nate normally didn't wish death on anyone, Daniel had deserved it.

With a sigh, he leaned back and watched the snow falling down outside the window. It was beautiful, but it was also like the sky was crying, its tears frozen on their way down. Between more and more bigger snowflakes, he saw something else slowly finding its way down and finally landing on their balcony, snow covering it.

Frowning, Nate got up and opened the door, not caring that it was damn freezing outside, and stretched his hand to grab the object he had seen.

"Nate! Close that door! It's cold!"

He turned around and closed the door behind him, still holding the object in his hand. When he brushed the snow off it, he realized it was a golden feather, soft to the touch. The sight of it pulled on his heart, even though he didn't know why.

"Are you okay?" Jamie asked. "You're crying."

Jamie came closer and looked at him, worried. Nate just shook his head and pressed the feather close to his body, tears dropping onto the floor as silent sobs escaped his lips. He didn't know what it meant, but he was sure it was important to him. He could feel it in his heart.

It was a hint of what he was missing so much—what had been taken from him.

APRIL 20TH, 2024

The last months had been hard. Nate had lived his life, cared for himself as much as he could. He had talked to his therapist about this feeling of missing something, and they tried to figure it out more, tried to find a way for Nate to still enjoy life.

He had taken Jamie's advice to go out more and was now in a club, his second drink in his hand, enjoying the music. He'd put the golden feather on a clip and made it into a pendant, wearing the necklace most of the time, hidden underneath his shirt. It felt good to have it so close to his heart. It gave him the feeling that he wasn't so alone anymore.

His gaze wandered to the small ring on his left hand, a cat-shaped head silhouette. He couldn't remember where he'd gotten it, but it invoked a similar feeling as the feather did.

Still, he felt empty, like something had been ripped out of him. Every morning, his bed felt too big for him, and the pain never dulled down.

"Hey, sorry for the direct approach, but would you dance with me?"

A little surprised, Nate turned around to the man who'd just asked him, even more surprised now. He was handsome and taller than him, with perfectly plucked dark eyebrows, wavy shoulder-length dark hair, and blue eyes that were hard to see in this light.

"Uhm, sure. I'm Nate."

With a big smile, the stranger took his hand and coaxed him onto the dance floor.

"Nice to meet you, Nate. My name's Rael. I'm sure we'll have a lot of fun together."

FEBRUARY 6TH, 2025

It had been almost a year since Nate had met Rael in this club, and they had gotten to know each other much more the last months. Rael was nice to him, treated him so much better than Daniel ever had—but he still couldn't fill the void in Nate's heart.

Nothing could.

Sighing, Nate leaned back in the plush armchair, a glass of absinthe in front of him on a rickety table, while he was just waiting for the movies to end so he could tidy up the cinema halls and head home. Sure, alcohol during work wasn't exactly allowed, but at this time, he was on his own, no one around but their projectionist, and he didn't care at all. As long as they got the job done drunk, no one bat an eye.

A bit absentmindedly, Nate scratched at the thick scar on his wrist. He didn't quite remember when he had cut himself so deep, he only knew it had been after one of the bad nights with Daniel. Neither could he remember how he had cared for the wound, or when he had gotten the small semicolon tattoo next to the thick scar. A lot of things in his mind were mushy, and he wondered if it was because of the alcohol.

With another sigh, Nate took a big sip of his drink, green and rich in flavor. Absinthe really was an experience and, what was more important, rather potent. Good thing his therapist didn't object anymore. Not since Nate had stopped going there because money was tight, and he had felt he was being patronized instead of helped all the time.

A quick glance at his phone revealed a message from Rael. He'd arrive in about ten minutes, to pick him up. It'd still leave him with almost half an hour of waiting for the movies. Groaning, Nate rubbed the palm of his hand against his temple, trying to make sense of his fucked up brain.

He should be happy. He had a wonderful best friend, a job with lots of freedom, and a caring boyfriend. Still, something was missing. The phone landed back on theleather-covered plate of the table with a thud and Nate leaned back, with his glass in hand, taking another sip.

Slowly, he pulled the necklace from under his longsleeved shirt, the golden feather dangling on it still as impeccable as the first time he'd seen it. He still wore it, every single day. It gave him a sense of security, the feeling he wasn't all alone and someone was watching over him. Why he felt this way, he didn't know. It was a strange thing, to be so connected to a single feather.

"Natey! What's that?" Rael threw himself into the armchair next to him, resulting in a protesting groan from said furniture, and grabbed the glass to sniff it. "Oh, absinthe? Fancy today?"

A grin hit him and Nate just shrugged. He hadn't even heard the creaking hinges of the swing doors, had been so distracted by the feather. Which he stuffed back under his longsleeved shirt now.

Rael didn't like seeing it for some reason, and Nate surely would never anger Rael.

After Rael had taken a big sip from his absinthe, he leaned closer, one hand on Nate's neck, to pull him into a firm kiss. He could feel the curve of Rael's full lips forming a smirk and when they parted, Nate could also see it.

"How long 'til your shift ends?"

Nate grabbed his phone to check the time and sighed. "Half an hour until the first movie ends." Still too much time, just sitting around here.

"How about you make another one of these and then we go upstairs and let time pass faster?" Rael suggested with a grin.

Of course Nate knew what he was hinting at, and although he wasn't very motivated right now, he didn't mind either. Slowly, he got up from his chair, a tiny bit wobbly on his feet, and headed behind the bar counter, to prepare yet another absinthe. In a very nontraditional way, and if anyone who actually enjoyed absinthe for the whole ritual saw him, they'd yell at him. Nate just chucked one cube of sugar into the dark green liquid, stirring it until it was dissolved, and filled the glass up with tap water, stirring it again, resulting in a light milky green mixture.

Rael had already gotten up and followed him to the bar, the half-full glass in his hand. It didn't stayhalf-full for long since Rael just downed it and put it next to the sink. "Come on! Don't have much time."

Nate nodded and took a sip from his fresh glass while he headed toward the door upstairs, to their breakroom-storage. He heard Rael's steps on the metal stairs behind him and when they were upstairs, he couldn't even put the glass aside when he already had Rael's hungry lips on his own.

Playlist

Higanbana – NUL.

Fallen Angel – Øfdream

My Demons (Acoustic) – STARSET

Die For You (Acoustic) – STARSET

Starlight (Acoustic) – STARSET

Point Of No Return (Acoustic) – STARSET

Dark On Me – STARSET

Let It Burn – Red

TRIALS – STARSET

The Truth Was Revealed – Walking Across Jupiter

Angel With A Shotgun – The Cab

Family – Badflower

Already Over – Red

Drowning – DØNTCALL

Higanbana and Nate hold a special place in my heart. It's been incredibly hard to write this story, but at the same time, it' been so rewarding and healing. Living with depression isn't easy, and I know from my own experiences what Nate goes through. To remind myself how far I've come—that I'm still *alive*—is an incredible achievement.

To everyone going through a similar pain, you're not alone. Please seek out the help you need because you deserve to be happy and experience joy again.

A special thanks goes out to my wonderful friends, whose books I referenced in some Easter eggs. We have *The Modern Mythos Anomaly* by Juniper Lake Fitzgerald in chapter 13 (Guardian). In chapter 19 (Nightmares), we have *Hymn of Memory* by S. Jean, and in chapter 22 (Worlds Apart), we have two books—*The Binding of Bloom Mountain* by Vesper Doom, and *Trick* by Cara Nox.

You're all amazing friends to me, and I'm glad to know all of you.

Acknowledgements

Thank you, Marek, for being an amazing friend. You've always been there for me through my darkest times, and you continue to support me. I'm incredibly glad and grateful to call you my friend. If you read this, I'm sorry—and I hope you didn't hear *my* voice again.

Thank you, Juniper, for the beautiful interior graphics once again.

A special thanks to Vernico, for all the helpful beta comments that really helped me form Higanbana into what it is now.

Thank you, bro, for being there for me from the very beginning (literally). You've always been my biggest supporter, and I love you endlessly. You'll always be the best big brother I could wish for.

Thank you, Ronove, for working on the paperback & e-book cover art and for your patience with me. It turned out so incredibly beautiful and makes this book gorgeous. Also, the character art included in this version were the first art of Nate and Raziel I had, and I love them dearly.

Also, a big thank you to Bei (Ante Kun) for the beautiful chibis you made for the characters of this book.

Thank you, Gabe, for your help editing the last draft and for polishing my words.

A big thanks to Starset, for being an incredible inspiration with so many songs.

And last but not least, a big thank you to all the ARC readers and anyone reading *Higanbana*. You're awesome!

If you're looking forward to more of Nate and Raziel—keep an eye out for the sequel!

Also by Jake Vanguard

Deity Chronicles

FIRST SNOW (MAY 2024)

FIRST ROSE (MAY 2025)

Angelverse

Higanbana (AUGUST 2024)

About the author

Jake Vanguard (he/they) is an indie author of queer dark fantasy, science fantasy, and a slice of horror and erotica. In his stories, he loves exploring queerness and contradictions, love and connections, family and friendship.

Their novels FIRST SNOW (Deity Chronicles 1) and HIGANBANA (Angelverse 1) were released 2024, with more to come.

instagram.com/jake.vanguard/

www.ingramcontent.com/pod-product-compliance
Lightning Source LLC
LaVergne TN
LVHW011004200726
843509LV00011B/978